BACK IN THE BACHELOR'S ARMS

VICTORIA PADE

SPECIAL EDITION

Published by Silhouette Books

America's Publisher of Contemporary Romance

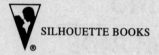

SILHOUETTE BOOKS

ISBN-13: 978-0-373-24771-4
ISBN-10:   0-373-24771-0

BACK IN THE BACHELOR'S ARMS

Printed in U.S.A.

"So do you think we can do this? Let bygones be bygones?"

Reid studied Chloe for a long moment with those brilliant green eyes.

"I can give it a try," he said when he finally did answer.

"I'd like that," Chloe said softly.

"I guess I'll see you tomorrow then. I'll be especially quiet until I know you're up."

She nodded.

"Good night, then."

"Get home safely," she joked, making him smile a little again.

For another moment they remained standing there, not too far apart, just looking at each other.

As they did, Chloe couldn't help recalling so many other times when they'd said good-night at the door much like that.

Only then he would have kissed her.

He would have kissed her in a way that would have filled her with a special kind of heat. That would have made her feel like his and his alone....

Dear Reader,

Welcome back to Northbridge! I hope it's beginning to feel as much like home to you as it is to me.

In this book Chloe Carmichael is making her own return—temporarily—to Northbridge, too. She isn't so happy to be there at first and that's actually how this book came into being. I love it there but I started to think about the good and the bad of a small town. About the people who stay and the people who don't. About why someone might leave somewhere this warm and friendly and fun (because I'd love to find my own Northbridge and I can't imagine leaving if I ever did). I started to think about the history, the memories we all carry around with us. About how sometimes there are secrets, too. And scars and old wounds that can make even the most ideal surroundings not so appealing. Then I threw Dr. Reid Walker into the mix—hot hunk with a hurt heart. Hmm…

Anyway, that's where this story came from. And along with it, you'll also learn a little more about the scandal that rocked Northbridge back in the sixties when Reverend Perry's wife Celeste ran off with the bank robbers. I still don't know all there is to know about that one but as it comes to me, I'll pass it along to you.

In the meantime, I wish you a pleasant visit to my little town, and I'll keep my fingers crossed that you enjoy it there as much as I do.

Happy reading!

Victoria

Books by Victoria Pade

VICTORIA PADE

is a native of Colorado, where she continues to live and work. Her passion—besides writing—is chocolate, which she indulges in frequently and in every form. She loves romance novels and romantic movies—the more lighthearted, the better—but she likes a good, juicy mystery now and then, too.

Chapter One

"**I**'ll see one more patient and then that's it for me for the next week—I'm on vacation as of midnight. So what's up?" Dr. Reid Walker asked the emergency room nurse he was working with.

"We only have one patient left, period," the nurse responded. "Second week of October, first snowstorm of the season, icy roads—she slid into a telephone pole just outside of town. She says she's fine but the air bag deployed and you know police policy around here—when the air bag inflates, they bring 'em into the E.R. to be checked out no matter what the vehicle occupant says. Her name is Chloe Carmichael."

Reid stopped short at that. "Say the name again."

"Chloe Carmichael," the nurse repeated. Then, without noticing the effect that particular name was having on Reid, she said, "I'll release our flu case, hopefully you can wrap up the car accident, and we're clear. Next shift will be in any minute. They can handle anything that comes in after this, and we're both outta here."

Reid didn't respond as the nurse left him. He also didn't move. Instead he stayed where he was, just outside the counter that surrounded the area that staff referred to as the fishbowl, where medical personnel convened to talk, pick up charts, get supplies and do paperwork.

The emergency room of the only medical facility in the small town of Northbridge, Montana, had just four rooms branching out from the fishbowl. Two of them were dark and unoccupied. Reid had just left the third after informing a girl from Northbridge College that she could relax, she wasn't pregnant and had only a case of influenza. Which left the fourth room the only possibility for the location of his next patient.

Chloe Carmichael.

Sunday night, 11:45. It was a hell of an end to the weekend. A hell of a beginning to his vacation.

Still, Reid didn't budge. He glanced across the fishbowl to Room 4.

The lights there were on. The wall facing the fishbowl was glass above the cupboards where gowns and necessary equipment were stored in each of the triage rooms. The privacy curtain wasn't completely pulled around the bed and there, in the small gap left, he could partially see the patient.

But partially was enough.

She was sitting up in the bed, dressed in a hospital gown, appearing none-the-worse-for-wear given that she'd just been in an automobile accident. Looking better, in fact, than the last time Reid had seen her.

Fourteen years ago.

She'd been seventeen.

He'd been eighteen.

It seemed like yesterday.

Chloe Carmichael.

Her family had moved to Northbridge when she was in elementary school. They'd lived a few doors down from the house Reid's family owned, the house where his mother still resided. The Carmichaels had lived there until fourteen years ago when they'd left town abruptly. They'd rented the house out ever since. A few months ago it had gone up for sale, and Reid and his brother Luke had put in an offer on it. Rental property in a college town was a good investment. Even if it was still connected to Chloe Carmichael.

Reid and Luke were about to close on the sale of the house she'd inherited from her parents. But Reid had been told that the Realtor would be acting as Chloe Carmichael's proxy because she didn't want to return to Northbridge.

So what was she doing here?

"Oh, good, you haven't gone in to see the other patient yet."

The nurse's voice caught him by surprise. Reid had been so lost in his own thoughts he hadn't been aware that she'd rejoined him.

"You were going to write a script for birth control pills so our college girl doesn't have any more pregnancy scares," the nurse reminded him.

Reid finally glanced back at the nurse. "Birth control pills. Right. Good invention."

"I think so," the nurse agreed in a puzzled tone of voice.

Reid didn't explain himself. He merely filled out and signed the prescription and handed the pad back to the nurse.

But even once she'd left him alone again he remained where he was, returning to his study of the room he was supposed to be going to.

The room where Chloe Carmichael awaited him.

She still had that wavy, licorice-black hair. Only as far as he could tell from his limited view, it was shorter now, ending just below her shoulders rather than falling to the middle of her back.

She still had the most flawless porcelain skin he'd ever seen—he could tell that even through the scant gap in the curtain. The softest, smoothest skin he'd ever touched.

She still had the straightest nose. The most luscious pink lips. And despite the fact that he couldn't see them because she was looking down at the bed, he had no doubt she also still had the biggest, bluest eyes....

No, those fourteen years hadn't harmed her any. They'd only made better what he'd thought was perfect before.

Damn it.

And just like that Reid flashed back to one of the last times he'd seen Chloe Carmichael—the beginning of the end for them....

It had been a night in early summer, in the front yard of that house that would be his and his brother's very soon. The house he and his mother and the town minister had been thrown out of. The house he'd been banned from. The house Chloe Carmichael had had to sneak out of to talk to him.

The memory was so vivid. The memory of cupping the soft skin of her beautiful face between his hands. Of kissing warm lips and tasting the salt of the tears that had brimmed from those eyes.

"I don't care what they say, this isn't the end of us. It's only the beginning. I'll make sure of it," he'd told her that night.

Big words. A lot of bravado. All for nothing.

Nothing but misery.

"What are you doing?" the nurse's voice intruded again. "I thought you wanted to get this over with so we could go home. But here you are. Are your feet glued to the floor or what?"

Reid didn't respond as the nurse entered the center of the fishbowl to do the paperwork that went with the release of the college girl.

He merely continued staring across the distance at the patient he was supposed to see. The patient who wasn't just another patient.

The patient who was Chloe Carmichael.

And it astounded him suddenly that that was all it took—her name, a glimpse of her, knowing he was about to come face-to-face with her again—to make old feelings spring to the surface.

Old, ugly feelings.

Red-hot anger.

And plenty of it.

Even after all these years…

* * *

"Dr. Walker will be in to see you soon...."

The nurse's words rang in Chloe Carmichael's ears as she nervously plucked the hospital bedcovers into pyramids.

Dr. Walker...

She wanted to hope that the Dr. Walker who was to examine her was from a different Walker family than the one she'd known growing up. The Walker family who had been her neighbors. Her friends. One of them more than just her friend.

But what were the odds that the Dr. Walker she was slated to see *was* a different Walker than the Walkers she'd known?

Not great, she thought.

At least the Walker family she was familiar with had been a big one. Five kids—Reid, Luke, Ad, Ben and Cassie. Cassie—the one girl.

Maybe I'll luck out and Dr. Walker is Cassie Walker—a woman doctor. All the better...

But while Chloe wouldn't be thrilled with being examined by Luke, Ad or Ben if one of them was the Walker who had become a doctor, she just hoped it wasn't Reid.

Please don't let it be Reid...

It was bad enough to be back in Northbridge, let alone in the emergency room there. But to be waiting for a doctor who might be Reid?

Just please, please, don't let it be Reid...

Northbridge and Reid.

The place she was afraid she could never come to again without feeling embarrassed and ashamed.

And the man who had grown from the boy she'd had to hurt.

Northbridge and Reid Walker and shame and embarrassment and pain and remorse—no, not a chapter in her life she wanted to revisit.

And she hadn't thought she would have to.

When her parents had been killed in a boating accident eleven months earlier, Chloe had inherited the house they'd all lived in in Northbridge. The house her parents had employed a Realtor to rent out since they'd all hurriedly left the small town.

But Chloe hadn't wanted any part of anything connected to Northbridge or her past and so, after considering the financial aspects of selling the place, she'd finally decided to do it.

The same Realtor who had handled the house as a rental property had put the place up for sale, assuring Chloe that selling the old house could be accomplished without Chloe's personal appearance in town. Which had been the plan.

But once the Realtor had buyers, she'd called.

There was some furniture, some clothes, some Carmichael belongings packed in boxes in the attic. Did Chloe want it all sent to her?

Chloe had considered it. She'd even looked into the cost of having it brought—sight unseen—to Arizona. But the cost was substantial and since she was unsure what she would want to keep and what she would merely throw away, it seemed unwise to bring everything to Tucson only to toss it out there. She needed to go through the things herself before paying to have anything shipped to her.

So she'd resigned herself to making this trip. She'd intended to slip into Northbridge, do what needed to be done at the house and slip out again, not attending the closing. No more than a few people would ever know she had been back where the events of fourteen years ago had been the talk of the town.

But now here she was, brought in by a police officer, her rental car in need of towing after being smashed into a pole. That was a commotion that would never go unnoticed in Northbridge. That was a story that would be told. And repeated. And repeated. Along with the fact that Chloe Carmichael had been behind the wheel.

That was certainly *not* slipping quietly in and out of Northbridge's back door.

Best-laid plans…

The curtain that was pulled most of the way around the bed opened just then and Chloe's eyes shot from the pyramided covers to the person who had thrown it wide.

She didn't need to read his hospital badge to know who he was, even though he'd changed considerably since she'd last seen him. She would have recognized those staggeringly handsome features anywhere. After all, the younger version of them had materialized in her mind's eye more times than she could count in the last fourteen years.

"Reid," she whispered more to herself than in greeting.

He took it as a greeting, though, and responded in kind, "Chloe."

Well, maybe *in kind* wasn't exactly accurate. There was nothing kind in that single utterance of her name. Clearly Reid Walker wasn't any happier to see her than she was to see him. In fact, if the grim expression on his face and the cutting tone of his voice were any indication, he was even more unhappy than she was. More than unhappy, actually. He seemed ticked off, disgusted, put out and all-round disgruntled.

Probably no more than she should have expected.

Chloe took a deep breath and tried to make the best of a bad situation. "It is you. The nurse said Dr. Walker would be in and I wondered if maybe Cassie or one of your brothers had ended up going to medical school. Or if it was you. Apparently it was you…"

"Apparently."

Snide. Sarcastic. Downright nasty.

This was not going to be nice.

His gaze dropped to the chart he held in his hands but Chloe had the sense that more than studying whatever was written on it, he just couldn't stand to look at her.

"Single?" he said after a moment, obviously reading what she'd marked on the papers she'd filled out. "Is there anybody you want notified of the accident? I know your parents are gone—"

"I appreciated the flowers and sympathy card your mom sent. I wondered how she knew—"

"The newspaper ran a small article," he explained curtly, still looking only at her chart and wasting no time going back to what he'd been saying. "Is there anyone else you want notified of the accident or asked to come here to be with you? Friends? Other family? A boyfriend or fiancé?"

Was he being persistent about that as a matter of course or was he trying to find out if she was unattached?

Given his attitude, Chloe thought it must be a matter of course.

"No, there's no boyfriend or fiancé or anyone else who I want called."

He didn't so much as nod to acknowledge her answer. He merely shot her another question. "Do you want to tell me what happened?"

For a split second she thought he was talking about what had happened fourteen years ago. But of course that wasn't the case and she realized it a little belatedly. She was in an emergency room. He was her doctor.

"The weather was fine when I left the Billings airport," she began to explain. "But about halfway here it started to snow. Hard. The roads iced up and even though I was driving at a snail's pace, the rental car spun out and I hit a telephone pole. The engine died. The doors wouldn't open. The air bag was in my face. I couldn't do anything but use my cell phone to dial 911 for help."

"Any loss of consciousness?"

"No. But the cop who finally got there had to pry one of the doors open to get me out. Once I *was* out, it didn't seem like any bones were broken or anything, but he insisted that he bring me here anyway."

Was she rambling? She was afraid she was. But she was so unnerved both by the accident and by seeing Reid again unexpectedly that she sort of didn't know which end was up.

"Are you having any pain?" he demanded, deigning to look at her again but with such scorn she wished he hadn't.

"No, not really. It kind of shook me up but like I said, I'm not hurt. The air bag took most of the impact. There are a couple of scrapes on my arms and a bruise on my knee, but otherwise, I'm fine."

"I'll still need to check you over."

He sounded as if he'd rather walk barefoot through toxic waste—she wasn't giving him high marks for bedside manner.

Not that Chloe was any more thrilled with the prospect of Reid Walker—of all people—examining her…

"There isn't another doctor?" she ventured.

"Molly, you want to come in here?" he hollered over his shoulder rather than answering Chloe's question.

The nurse she'd seen before joined them.

"Is the next shift in yet?" he demanded.

"No," the nurse answered. "And they may be a while. This storm took everybody off guard—J.T. just called and his car won't start so he's walking in. I'd just hung up from talking to him when Shauna called to say her husband had to go out to deal with a frozen water main and she's having to find someone to come stay with the kids before she can leave home."

Reid stabbed Chloe with another glance. "And if you want to wait for them you should know that you won't be seeing a doctor. Shauna is a nurse and J.T. is a nurse-practitioner—they do our overnights and call for help if something too serious for them to handle comes in. Or I can do the exam but have Molly stay in the room, if that makes you more comfortable. Your choice."

Nothing in the world could make Chloe more comfortable at that moment. All she wanted was to get this over with and slink away from the entire situation. And waiting for another shift to come in in a snowstorm didn't seem like the fastest route to that.

"What will you have to do?" she asked before she committed to anything.

"I'll check for head, neck and spinal cord injuries. Check your extremities—" He paused to address the nurse once more. "Did you look for seat belt signs?"

"I did. There weren't any," the nurse responded.

"Seat belt signs?" Chloe inquired.

"If there's been a lot of force against the restraint of the seat belt and there's bruising, that can be an indication of internal injury," he said as if any idiot should know that.

"The seat belt unsnapped itself before the accident ever happened. I'd had to take it off. I guess it was lucky the air bag came up when it did."

"Then we don't need to worry about injury from the seat belt, do we?"

More sarcasm before the unpleasant physician continued outlining the exam he would need to perform on her.

"I'll listen to your abdomen with the stethoscope, apply some pressure to see if that causes you pain you might not otherwise be aware of, listen to your heart and lungs. I can do everything on the outside of the gown and I'll be as hands-off as possible. Believe me, I'll be as hands-off as possible."

Because he didn't want to touch her.

And she didn't want him to touch her.

Did she?

Of course she didn't.

So why was it so insulting that he seemed to abhor the idea?

It just was, that's all. But Chloe tamped down on that to deal with what she was being forced to deal with. "And it won't take long?" she asked.

"Not one split second longer than it has to."

So not only didn't he want to touch her, he didn't want anything between them prolonged either—that was the message he was relaying.

"Okay," Chloe conceded reluctantly.

"Shall I go or stay?" the confused-sounding nurse asked then.

"Stay!" both Chloe and Reid said at the same time.

Then Reid added, "Definitely stay."

As he went to the nearby sink and washed his hands the nurse stepped to the side of the bed, smiling reassuringly but still appearing as if she didn't understand what was going on.

But then she'd already told Chloe that she was new in town. Which meant that she likely didn't know that once upon a time Chloe and Reid had been teenagers madly in love with each other.

Until Chloe had turned up pregnant.

And all hell had broken loose.

Chapter Two

Monday morning came to life with a clear blue sky full of sunshine falling on more than two feet of pristine white snow. And Reid was there to see it all because he was awake and out of bed and watching the day break as he stood at the picture window in the living room of the house he and Luke owned together and shared. Directly across the street from the Carmichael house they were about to buy.

But it wasn't the sunrise or the snow that was on Reid's mind at that early hour. It was Chloe Carmichael and himself and the past and the present and what a mess everything seemed to have turned into again in the blink of an eye.

It was also the fact that he knew he'd earned a swift kick in the ass for his behavior the night before.

Fourteen years ago Chloe Carmichael, together with her parents, had taught him a harsh lesson in frustration and helplessness.

But fourteen years was a long time. And in the early hours of the morning, once his unreasonable anger had subsided somewhat, he'd decided he wasn't proud of the way he'd acted the previous evening. And he definitely wasn't proud of the way he'd treated Chloe professionally.

In fact, while behaving like a scorned adolescent was dumb, not doing what he should have as a doctor was inexcusable.

Okay, so he didn't think that he'd missed anything during the exam or that Chloe actually had been more hurt than she'd seemed to be. He'd seen enough accident victims to recognize the difference between severe injuries and minor ones like the scrapes on her arms and the bruise on her leg.

But still, he'd gone about the examination at the same inept level he'd gone about his very first patient exam in medical school—he'd been as reluctant to actually put his hands on her as some rookie.

It was just that touching Chloe even slightly had shot him back to a time when touching her, kissing her, holding her, had been almost the only things he'd ever thought about. It hadn't been something he could do professionally—medically—without remembering that. Without reliving it.

Without wanting even now to do more of it. In a private setting. And in a way that had absolutely nothing to do with his job.

Inexcusable, unacceptable, unwarranted and inappropriate.

And it sure as hell wasn't the kind of physician he was. Any more than being a surly SOB was the kind of man he was.

Which led him to the conclusion that this had to be fixed.

Not that he was looking to be overly friendly toward Chloe Carmichael at this juncture. Or to rekindle anything. He'd done his damnedest to do the right thing fourteen years ago and it had blown up in his face; he didn't want to get into anything with her again now.

But as long as she was in Northbridge, as long as he was in the situation he'd discovered when he'd arrived home last night, he'd rather have a temporary coexistence with Chloe that was amicable. And in order for it to be amicable, he knew he had to rise above his old wounds and make the best of things as they were right now.

"Hey. What're you doing up so early?"

Reid's brother surprised him from behind and Reid turned to find Luke obviously just out of bed, padding in on bare feet from the bedrooms down the hall.

"You won't believe it when I tell you," Reid responded, leaning one shoulder against the cold glass.

"The snow? It was falling before I went to sleep," Luke said with a nod towards the big plate glass window that was bracing Reid's weight.

"Not the snow. What the snow brought in with it."

"Yeah? What did the snow bring in with it?" Luke asked.

"Chloe Carmichael," Reid said as if he were dropping a bomb.

Bomb enough to wake up Luke. His eyes opened wide beneath arched brows and for a moment he was gape-jawed before he said, "Chloe Carmichael? She's here? In Northbridge?"

Reid inclined his head at the window, too. "Not only in Northbridge. She's across the street. Apparently staying at the house."

Luke grimaced and let out an expletive as he joined Reid to look out at their soon-to-be rental property.

If Luke had been expecting to see signs of Chloe he was disappointed. There weren't any to see. Which prompted him to say, "How do you know?"

"She ended up in my emergency room at midnight after hitting a telephone pole."

"Was she hurt?"

"No," Reid said. "Scrapes and bruises, but that's it. At least I hope that's it. I didn't do as thorough an exam as I probably should have."

"I need coffee," Luke said as if he were suddenly desperate for the stuff and headed for the kitchen that was through an archway to the rear of the living room.

Reid finally gave up the spot he'd maintained at the window for nearly an hour and followed his brother, refilling his own mug once Luke had poured his. Then they both sat on vinyl chairs at the chrome and Formica kitchen table that had been in their mother's basement for decades before they'd confiscated it for use in their own place.

"You're not going to get sued for malpractice, are you?" Luke asked then.

"I'm reasonably sure she was okay."

"And she's at the house?"

"Surprise!"

"I guess. Did you tell her we were working on it?"

Betty, the Realtor, had given them the okay and the key. Betty had explained to them that Chloe had made it clear she didn't want to be bothered with anything to do with the house or the sale. She'd given Betty written permission to hire any workmen of Betty's choosing to do the necessary repairs and replacements to facilitate the process.

Betty had given Reid and Luke the option of doing the work themselves so that it was done to their specifications. She'd said that she was killing two birds with one stone—Chloe would have less expense because Reid and Luke would not charge for labor, and Reid and Luke would have things done the way they wanted, and in time for their renters to move right in after the closing.

Betty had warned them that they could be taking a risk, that if the sale didn't go through for some reason their time could be wasted. But since no one doubted that the deal would close, Reid and Luke had decided to take that risk.

"I didn't say anything about the house," Reid told his brother. "I wasn't really…nice."

Luke frowned. "How not-nice were you? Like not-nice enough that Chloe might pull out of the deal?"

"She wants to sell. I doubt she'll nix it just because I was unfriendly." Unfriendly in the extreme—but Reid didn't see any reason to worry his brother by elaborating. "Besides, we have a contract and the downpayment is in escrow—she can't back out just because I was a little...disagreeable."

"Not nice, unfriendly *and* disagreeable," Luke said as if Reid was alarming him anyway.

"Let's just say that I wasn't particularly neighborly," Reid amended. "For instance, I probably should have asked where she was staying and offered to drive her since her car was out of commission from the accident, but—"

"You didn't."

"No. Instead, Molly stepped in and offered her a lift, and then it was like some kind of caravan because there we were, the only two cars on the road, me driving right behind them until we got here. Where I pulled into our driveway and Molly let Chloe off across the street—"

"So that's how you know she's over there."

"Right. We ended up in some kind of synchronized arrival, walked up to the front doors at the same time, opened them, looked over at each other and then went in and closed the doors as if we didn't even know each other. Molly must have thought I was crazy and it's a good thing she didn't have to go out of her way to get here or I would have felt bad about her driving in the snow when it ended up that I could easily have brought Chloe with me."

"But Molly's been in town only a few months. She doesn't know anything about you and Chloe Carmichael."

"She knew something was up. She couldn't have missed it at the hospital."

Luke nodded. "Why is Chloe here? Betty said she

was firm about not wanting to come in for the closing and even that isn't until a week from today."

"I don't know why she's here. I stuck strictly to the medical stuff."

"You didn't ask *why* she was here and you didn't even know she planned to stay at the house until you saw her go in?"

"Yeah, I know, those were probably things I should have gotten into. But I didn't. I wasn't in the mood." Plus none of it had occurred to him until he'd seen her go into the house across the street because at the hospital he'd been so wrapped up in old resentments and anger that he hadn't been able to think about anything except what touching her had done to him....

"How's she look?" Luke asked then as if he'd read Reid's mind.

"Freaking fantastic," Reid blurted out before he even realized he was going to admit it.

It made Luke laugh but only barely before he caught himself. "What did you expect if you ever saw her again? That she would've grown warts?"

"Warts are no more than she deserved," Reid muttered, hating that the simple question about how Chloe looked put her image right back into his head again after he'd fought numerous times through the night to get it out.

Damn her, anyway, for *not* having warts. For looking even better in full view than she had through the gap in the privacy curtain. For that gleaming black hair that waved around her alabaster skin like a picture frame. For those take-a-second-glance features that made her cute and striking and amazingly beautiful depending on her expression. For those straight white teeth and that smile—that smile that had shown itself only nervously last night—that was still bright enough to light a dark room. For those eyes that were the color of freshly washed summer blueberries. For that tight, compact little body on that barely five-foot-two-inch frame and those smallish breasts that had been the first ones he'd ever felt....

Just damn her, anyway, for haunting him!

"Okay, so she looks good," Luke said then. "Was she as *unfriendly* to you as you were to her?"

"No. I was the only jerk in the room. She was fine. Not thrilled with me being her doctor, but what else can you expect?"

"So she was nice enough and you were *still* a jerk?"

"Yep."

Luke shrugged. "Well, she *does* have some of that coming. I just wish it had come *after* the closing instead of before we get there. She didn't give you any idea why she's here?"

"I don't think it's for old times' sake," Reid snapped.

"What do we do now? Call Betty, have her go over and talk to Chloe? Smooth whatever feathers you might have ruffled?"

Reid already knew what he had to do. As a doctor and as a man. So he was prepared for that question and shook his head.

"I'll wait for a decent hour and then I'm going to have to go myself. I need to make sure she's still okay from the accident. I'll apologize for not having my party face on last night, and maybe that'll smooth any ruffled feathers."

Luke didn't jump at that solution. Instead his concerns now were obviously for Reid.

"Can you do that? Are you sure you *want* to?"

"I think I have to," Reid admitted quietly. "For the sake of the sale, the renters and myself. I didn't like me much last night."

Luke nodded as if he understood. "It couldn't have been easy for you to see her again. I know you had doubts about whether or not you wanted to live across the street from the Carmichaels' old place fourteen months ago, and more doubts now about buying their old place. I know that I had to twist your arm to even get you in that door again when it came on the market."

"No, it wasn't easy to see Chloe again. Especially when I didn't expect it and wasn't prepared," Reid acknowledged at least that much of what his brother had said. "But she's here, we're all tied up with the house and the sale and her as a result, and I'll do what I have to. Besides, like I said, I'd better make sure she's okay health-wise and that I didn't miss something in the exam last night."

"You're sure? I mean, I know I took off work last week to play carpenter but I might be able to arrange something for this week, too, if you just can't face her."

Reid shook his head. "Last week was vacation-with-pay. If you took off this week, too, you'd have to do it on your own dime and I know you can't afford that. Especially now, with this new mortgage hanging over our heads. Plus there's my substitute coming in from Billings who would have to be compensated for his time and trouble and the trip here even if I have him turn around and go back. And I'm really not so spineless that I can't face an old girlfriend."

"I never said you were spineless. I don't know if I could be anything but a bastard to Chloe Carmichael if I were in your shoes. And she was more than just an old girlfriend to you."

"Still, I'll do what needs to be done to get to the closing on the house. I'll make sure I'm not in line for a malpractice suit, and then hopefully whatever Chloe came to Northbridge for won't keep her here long. With any luck she'll get the hell out of town before we know it, and I won't ever have to see her again for the rest of my life—that's the incentive."

Luke didn't seem convinced. "And you don't have any feelings for her?"

"Only bad ones," Reid said without hesitation.

And he counted as bad feelings the stirring he'd felt when he'd touched her and the fact that the revised mental picture of her had somehow etched itself indelibly on his brain.

Because in no way were they things he *wanted* to experience.

Chloe was not operating at top speed Monday morning. Car accident. Encountering Reid Walker. Having even a cursory physical exam performed by him. Finding when the nurse drove her home that Reid lived directly across the street. Having to clean the upstairs bathroom before she could use it. Needing to turn the mattress on the double bed in her room before covering it with two mattress pads, clean sheets, blanket and pillows she'd brought with her in order to be comfortable using things that had been the domain of college students for many years. And then having images of Reid climbing into that bed with her. All together it hadn't made for a restful night's sleep. Or for a relaxing lounge in bed when she'd awakened.

No, she was up by 7:20 a.m. to discover that her entire body was very stiff—no doubt a side effect of the accident.

The stiffness eased when she moved around though. And she did that because it had been so late when she'd arrived that she hadn't explored all that was going on in the house. And she wanted to.

The living room was nearly finished being painted. There was a roll of new carpeting against a wall, waiting to be laid. Drapes had disappeared. The furniture her parents had left so the place could be considered furnished was gone. And only a single pole lamp with a bare bulb stood in one corner to provide some light after dark.

Luckily the new locks were merely near the front door and hadn't yet been installed or she wouldn't have been able to get in.

The first-floor bathroom had a new sink and toilet installed and had also been painted, as had the two bedrooms upstairs, where the carpeting had been removed and the hardwood floors refinished.

The kitchen was apparently next—and last—on the agenda once the living room was completed because there were tarps, rolls of masking tape and cans of paint waiting. Boxes of ceramic tile were also stacked in the corner to replace the linoleum and the backsplash, and the refrigerator was stocked with nothing but beer and soda.

And everywhere there were remnants of construction and cleanup that had apparently been left for the end with foam coffee cups, soda cans and beer bottles set here and there and forgotten.

Like finding Reid Walker to be her emergency room doctor, the house was not what Chloe had expected, and once she knew what was underway, she called her Realtor.

Betty.

Of course Betty was stunned to learn that Chloe had come into town. Why wouldn't she be when Chloe had been adamant about not wanting any involvement in what was going on here?

"I was surprised to find the extent of the work already done and in progress on the house, though," Chloe told the other women after explaining why she'd decided to see what was in the attic before paying to have it all shipped to Arizona.

"I've been e-mailing you step by step and you've authorized the cost of the materials," Betty said.

"I guess I just wasn't keeping track." Probably because she'd wanted to dispense of anything that brought Northbridge to mind as quickly as possible, paying as little attention to it as she could manage, and then forgetting about it. "But I know I told you the maximum I was willing to spend on this and after seeing the extent of the work I'm a little worried that you aren't staying within my budget."

"All the work was necessary—as I told you when we spoke before, years of renters had taken a toll on the place. But we'll actually come in under your budget because with Luke and Reid doing the work there aren't any labor charges."

"Luke and Reid are doing the work? You didn't tell me that!"

"I did. I've kept copies of all my e-mails to you and that was one of the first. You didn't answer it, but I thought that since you'd left it to me to choose whatever handymen or workmen were required, you didn't care and didn't feel the need to respond."

Betty went on to explain the advantages of the arrangement to all parties but Chloe only heard it peripherally. Her mind was stalled on one thing: Reid Walker was doing the work on the house.

It was only when Betty began to talk about how Reid had taken vacation time this week to finish the job that Chloe tuned in again.

"He'll be *here?* All week? While *I'm* here?" she demanded of the Realtor.

Harshly, apparently, because Betty stopped short and there was only silence on the other end of the line for a long moment.

And when Betty spoke again her tone was cool and clipped. "Yes, Reid is scheduled to be there all week. Which I would have been happy to tell you had you let me know you were coming into town and intended to stay at the house. But you were very clear about how much you *didn't* want to be anywhere near here."

That was true. And that had been her intention. And because she'd wanted to simply slip into town without drawing any attention to herself she hadn't informed her Realtor.

"Can that be changed?" Chloe asked then. "Reid working on the house this week? Can I say no?"

"Well, of course that would be your prerogative but it would hardly be fair to—"

The doorbell rang just then.

Chloe wanted to scream with frustration. But she knew this was all her fault. Her own fault for not having paid close attention to Betty's e-mails. For not having let the Realtor know she was coming to Northbridge.

And screaming wouldn't accomplish anything and neither was this phone call.

"Someone is at the door. I'll just deal with this," Chloe said, cutting off the guilt-trip the woman was laying on her, and hanging up so she could move to the door.

Chloe hadn't showered yet. She hadn't done anything with her hair since getting up, so the ponytail she'd put it in before going to bed was lopsided and spilling strands of hair. She was wearing what she'd slept in—a pair of pajama pants and a T-shirt that weren't revealing in the slightest, but that also weren't what she wanted to be wearing to answer the door.

On the second ring of the bell, however, she realized there was nothing she could do about her appearance and answered it anyway.

To find Reid, who was standing on the front porch holding two steaming cups of coffee.

He held one of them aloft and said, "Truce?"

"Are we at war?" Chloe asked, trying not to notice how good he looked standing there in a pair of ancient jeans and a plain white crew-necked T-shirt under a jean jacket.

There was more form to him dressed in those clothes than had been in evidence in his hospital scrubs the night before and she couldn't help noticing that his shoulders were broader and more muscular than they had been years ago. His biceps seemed to fill his jacket sleeves to capacity.

His chest was expansive beneath the T-shirt, narrowing to a waist and hips that were taut and toned, easing into thighs massive enough not to leave any spare room in those jeans.

Plus, unless she was mistaken, he was a couple of inches taller than the six feet he'd sported at eighteen. All of which made him very imposing, coffee-truce in hand or no coffee-truce.

"I don't want to be at war, no," he was saying in answer to her question as she forced her attention away from cataloguing the attributes of the man's body that were vastly improved over that of the boy's. "But I think I sort of mounted the first attack last night, so I wouldn't blame you if you're arming yourself for the second."

Chloe considered how to handle this. He might have had the advantage the night before but it was on her side now. She could take it and give him a taste of his own medicine, or she could choose the high ground.

But being in Northbridge, in the same house, seeing him again, was bad enough. Fighting with him would only make it worse. So she decided on the high ground.

"I'll take the coffee," she said, reaching for the cup.

"Can we talk?" he asked as she took her first sip.

A slight frown beetled his brow but this time she didn't think for even a moment that he was referring to talking about what had happened fourteen years ago. Instead she was reasonably certain the house and what was going on with it was more what he had in mind.

Chloe stepped out of the way of the door as an invitation. "Looks like we'd better," she said, pointedly glancing at the disarray of the living room that the front door opened into.

Reid accepted the invitation, closing the door behind himself. When he had, he nodded in the same direction. "Luke and I have been working on the place."

"So I understand. I just got off the phone with Betty. She tells me you plan to work here all week."

"Yeah, that was the plan."

"And since you saw me get dropped off here last night you thought maybe you should be a little nicer to me so I'd agree to let you go through with it."

"Actually, no," he said very matter-of-factly. "When I saw Molly drop you off here last night I went in and kicked the couch and cussed for a while. It wasn't until after that that I decided—and not because of the remodel plan, but for other reasons—that I needed to come over this morning and start again. So, let me do that by backing up and asking if you're okay. Physically."

"I'm fine."

"Seriously? Because I can't say that was the best exam I've ever done and by now the doc from Billings who's filling in for me this week should be at the hospital. He could do a recheck. I wouldn't have to have anything to do with it."

"Seriously, I'm fine. I was stiff when I got out of bed, but even that's better."

"No bruises that appeared overnight? No abdominal pain? No nausea? No headache or neckache? No difficulty breathing when you went to bed or going up or down the stairs? No—"

"No nothing. I'm fine and I don't need the Billings doctor to confirm that. I was probably not even going ten miles an hour when I hit that pole. If the cop hadn't insisted, I wouldn't have gone in to a hospital at all."

Reid nodded slowly, as if he wanted to believe her reassurance but was still skeptical.

Then he said, "If you're absolutely sure you're all right, then it's a relief. I'm ordinarily not that lousy a doctor."

"You were pretty lousy," Chloe couldn't resist confirming just because it was obviously bothering him and she thought she'd earned at least that much retribution for his bad attitude the previous evening.

"And," he continued, "I should have asked where you were staying, I should have offered you a ride to wherever you needed to go. I was a jerk."

"Yes, you were."

"But this isn't easy for me. You have to know that."

"It isn't easy for me, either," she countered quietly, somberly.

That seemed to bring about a stalemate and silence reigned for longer than Chloe was comfortable with.

When she got too uncomfortable, she ended it.

"So, you're really needing to work here this week," she said to get back on the track they were both better able to deal with.

"I'm afraid I do. Northbridge has some support medical staff, but I'm the only doctor in town. I don't get a lot of vacations and when I do take one, it's complicated and really tough to back out on after everything has been set into motion. And our renters really need to get in as soon as it's humanly possible, and we've promised that the minute we close the place it will be ready for them. I know it's inconvenient for you, but Betty didn't say anything about you coming—"

"Betty didn't know."

"Well, we're in a bind."

Guess you shouldn't have been so contrary to me...

It was on the tip of Chloe's tongue but she didn't say it. After all, his scorn of the night before wasn't altogether uncalled for. And if accommodating the work he needed to get done on the house would put that scorn and contempt in check so she didn't have to deal with it while she was in Northbridge, she knew it was for the best.

"It looks like you'd be mainly working downstairs," she said with a question in her tone.

"I would be."

"I suppose I *should* have let Betty know I'd decided to do it, but I came to go through the stuff in the attic. I need to know what should be moved and what can just be thrown out. But with you down here and me up there, there would be a whole floor between us so maybe we wouldn't get in each other's way."

"We probably wouldn't."

"I guess it might be okay," she finally concluded, sounding hesitant, but less hesitant than she felt.

"I appreciate that," he said. Although getting what he wanted seemed to be double-edged.

Then he added, "If you *are* feeling all right, I'll leave and give you a little breathing room to get your day started. There are some supplies I need to pick up at the hardware store and I won't be losing much time if I come back in a couple of hours."

"That would be good," Chloe said.

"Okay then."

Reid hadn't moved more than a few steps from the door and he retraced those steps to open it again.

But before he went outside, he hesitated and glanced back at her from over one big, broad shoulder. "You're sure you don't have any signs of physical problems from the accident?"

"Positive."

He nodded but his gaze remained on her anyway for another moment before he actually did go out and close the door behind him.

Leaving Chloe with the image of his face branded on her brain as if it were the first time she'd ever seen him.

The image of a bone structure that fourteen years had honed to look as if it had been carved out of Italian marble, complete with high cheekbones that dropped to hollow cheeks, which gave him a rugged, outdoorsy appearance. A rugged, outdoorsy appearance enhanced by a jaw that was sharply defined and his mink-colored hair that was cut very short and left bristly all over.

The image of a straight, square forehead, and an aquiline nose that was only slightly long and added to the manly appeal of a face that was undeniably one of the most handsome she'd ever seen. The image of lips that were thin enough to be masculine and still full enough to be sensual. Of great eyes that were vibrant green tinged with only a hint of blue around the edges.

Deep, penetrating, intelligent eyes that had once been warm, caring and sensitive rather than cold, remote, guarded and wary as they had been last night and again this morning even in the midst of making peace.

No, seeing Reid, being in the same house with him, putting up a good front, wasn't going to be easy.

But even more difficult for her, Chloe thought, was resisting the urge to do something—anything—to make those eyes look at her the way they had so long ago, rather than the way they looked at her now.

Chapter Three

Chloe wasn't sure exactly what time Reid returned that afternoon. When he wasn't there by one-thirty she left a note propped against the outside of the front door telling him to just come in without ringing the bell because she might be on the phone. Then she went upstairs to her bedroom and called the rental car company where she'd encountered only problems.

But sometime during the two hours she was on the phone and mostly waiting, she heard water run downstairs and realized that Reid actually had come back.

And knowing that gave her conflicting emotions.

On the one hand it made her tense.

On the other hand, she became aware of a tiny flicker of excitement that she tried to expunge by concentrating on the difficulties she was having on the telephone.

But despite the fact that the difficulties were many and varied, they didn't dim that flicker that was still alive at four o'clock when she finally got off the phone.

Four o'clock was a late start on the attic and the thought of Reid being nearby made her consider not doing any work at all today.

Maybe she should just go downstairs to say hello, she thought.

And get another glimpse of him.

It was tempting. It could even be her contribution to the truce, she told herself.

But she knew she was only making excuses to see him and that that was not an inclination she should give in to. So, in the end, she decided that a late start was better than no start and went to the attic.

What she found there was hardly what she expected. She hadn't realized that her parents had accumulated— and left—quite that much stuff. Boxes upon boxes upon boxes were filled to the spilling point. There were two old trunks that were equally as packed, and an ancient bureau, a matching armoire and an aged wooden icebox that were all crammed full, too.

Plus the entire attic was covered in cobwebs and dust that made Chloe sneeze and warned her that the first thing she needed to do was clean away some of the yuck before she'd be able to spend the hours and hours it was going to require for her to sort through so much.

Luckily the old vacuum cleaner her parents had left in case the renters didn't have one was still in the hall closet of the second floor. It was also fortunately in working order.

She dragged it to the attic and went about the first order of business—cleaning enough to be able to stand it up there, firmly setting her thoughts to that rather than to Reid.

At least as much as possible knowing all the while that he was just downstairs....

It took the rest of the day and well into the evening before the attic and the surfaces of what was stored there were cobweb-, dust- and spider-free. Only when Chloe was done did she realize that the daylight that had been coming in through the octagonal windows at either end of the attic had disappeared and left only darkness outside.

And for no reason she understood, Reid was the first thing to pop into her mind again when it occurred to her that the day was gone.

With the second floor between them, she hadn't been able to hear anything, so she wondered if he was still downstairs or if he'd wrapped up his work for the day and left. Without a word to her.

And while she knew that was what she should be hoping for, as she turned off the bare bulbs that lit the attic and descended the narrow staircase to the second level, she wasn't hoping for that. Although she wasn't sure *what* she was hoping for...

Just in case he might still be there, she made a pit stop in her bedroom and the bathroom connected to it. The sweatsuit she'd put on earlier was covered in grime. Though she'd worn the less-than-attractive outfit so as not to run the risk of appearing as if she cared how she looked to Reid, she was secretly happy for the excuse to change and shed the sweats quickly, replacing them with jeans and a turtleneck T-shirt she tucked into them.

Then she went into the bathroom, washed her face, applied a hint of mascara and blush she'd also forgone earlier, and brushed out her hair. If she went downstairs and discovered Reid was long gone and she was alone, she was going to feel ridiculous for doing it all.

She was spared that, though. Because when she went down the second set of stairs, there was Reid, drying off a paintbrush.

"I didn't know if you were still here or not," Chloe said to announce herself, taking instant stock of him.

He was dressed in the same jeans and T-shirt he'd been wearing early that morning and there was a shadow of a beard darkening the lower half of that face that she wanted to study but knew she shouldn't. The shadow of a beard that gave him a scruffy, sexy appeal he would never have had at eighteen when there was too much of the boy still on the surface.

"I just wrapped it up for the day," he answered, his tone again amiable, if slightly restrained.

But then, as if he couldn't maintain that restraint, he nodded in the direction of the kitchen and said, "There's nothing to eat around here. What were you thinking about for dinner?"

"I hadn't thought about it yet," she admitted. Which was true. She'd eaten before leaving Billings the night before, assuming she would do a grocery run today. But without a car and feeling a bit too wobbly to walk to

Main Street, she'd lunched on the cheese crackers she'd brought with her. Then she'd been too busy fighting with the rental agency, cleaning the attic and thinking about Reid to consider what she was going to do for the evening meal.

"No car, no food in the house—how about ordering a pizza?" Reid said. "Paul's delivers now. It's one of Northbridge's flashy new amenities. I'll even treat."

"Really?" Chloe was so surprised by that offer that the word slipped out on its own. She just couldn't believe he was asking her to have dinner.

"Really," Reid confirmed. "We can do that, can't we? After all this time? Share a friendly pizza? It shouldn't be a big deal, should it?"

It probably shouldn't have been. But it was. At least to Chloe. It was a big deal that he was suggesting it, that he was willing to do it. And it was a big deal that she would be spending some time with him when he was making an effort to be pleasant. When he was likable. When he looked the way he did even in clothes that had paint smudges on them....

"Sure," she said after another moment's hesitation. "I think we can share a pizza. We're two grown up, civilized people." Who were both obviously only tentatively feeling their way along what was a new path for them.

"Let's do it then," he said. "Do you still want 'The Works' or have you gone vegetarian or something?"

Chloe knew from their high school days that the only pizzeria in town—Paul's Pizzeria—made a pie called The Works and that it was a large pizza topped with pepperoni, sausage, seasoned ground beef, black olives, mushrooms, green peppers, onions and three different kinds of cheese. It had been their favorite and at that moment it sounded wonderful.

"No, I haven't gone vegetarian or anything. The Works would be great," she said.

Reid set his paintbrush and rag down, then retrieved his cell phone from the pocket of his jean jacket where it was slung over the carpet roll. It took him only a few moments to order. He clearly recognized Paul's voice, identified himself, and said he wanted The Works sent to the rental house. In Northbridge everyone knew everyone else's business so intimately that that was all the information necessary.

Then Reid hung up. "We're all set. Luke and I have the fridge stocked with sodas and beer. Which would you like?"

Before Chloe could tell him, his cell phone rang.

"Why don't you tell me what *you* want and I'll get drinks while you answer that?" Chloe said.

"Soda is fine for me," he said by way of conceding the logic in that idea.

Chloe couldn't help overhearing the conversation as she took two colas from the refrigerator. While the tone was medical, there was something else about the exchange that sparked her interest.

When the call ended she went as far as the archway between the living room and the kitchen with cans in hand and said, "Linoleum or paint-splotched carpeting?" Since there weren't any chairs anywhere they would need to sit on the floor of one room or the other.

"Paint-splotched carpeting," he decreed, motioning

for her to sit in the very center where the least of the splatters marred the olive green shag floor covering.

Chloe sat with her legs curled to one side, watching as Reid returned his phone to his coat pocket, and trying—really, really trying—not to watch him do it and notice that even his derriere had improved with age.

"I didn't mean to eavesdrop on your call but…well, I did anyway. Do you deal in blood that *isn't* human?" she asked, referring to something she'd overheard him say.

He didn't join her on the floor. Instead, he went to stand with his back braced against the door, raising a knee so that the sole of one cowboy-booted foot was flat against the wooden panel. Then he slid his hands into the rear pockets that she'd been attempting not to look at a split second before.

"Remember the stories that have been around forever about Reverend Perry's wife?" Reid asked rather than giving her a direct answer about the blood.

"The *scandal* about her helping two itinerant farmhands rob the bank and running off with them?" Chloe said with intrigue in her tone.

"That would be the story, yes."

It was one of the biggest scandals to ever hit North-bridge. It had happened in 1960. Celeste Perry had reputedly grown weary of her righteous life as the wife of the town minister and the mother of their two young sons. She'd become enamored of one of two hard-living, hard-drinking farmhands—Frank Dorian and Mickey Rider—who had come into town during harvest season. On a night at the end of that October she'd slipped out of her marital bed to meet up with her lover and his partner. Later investigation had revealed that her lover and his partner were bank robbers rather than migrant farm workers, and after breaking into Northbridge's only Savings and Loan and its vault, and cleaning out all the money they could carry, the reverend's wife and the two men had disappeared.

"Is Reverend Perry still around?" Chloe asked, not only because she was curious, but also because it helped to have something to talk about that was completely separate from either of them and their own past problems, and she wanted to prolong it.

"He is," Reid answered. "But he retired about five years ago."

"And your phone call had something to with him and what happened with his wife?"

"We're refurbishing the north bridge—it's being restored and the land around it will be turned into a park so the town's namesake isn't just some rundown relic. Anyway, a couple of weeks ago one of the guys working on it found an old duffel bag jammed into the rafters. It was stuffed with the belongings of one of the robbers and the empty moneybags from the bank. There were some stains on the outside of the duffel that looked like they might be blood."

"*Human* blood," Chloe repeated.

"There's no way to tell that just by looking at it. Especially after all this time. I did the initial tests—"

"*You* did?"

"The wearing-of-many-hats in a small town. The police department keeps some of the chemicals needed to do the initial tests. The first thing that has to be determined is if it *is* human blood—if it proves to be animal blood they don't bother the forensic lab in Billings and waste their time. I did the tests here and they appeared positive for human blood."

"But that call sounded as if someone else was telling you that."

"They were confirming it and expanding on it," he qualified. "The call was from the forensic lab—I've been playing phone tag with the pathologist there since this morning and that was him returning my last message to his voice mail. I was right, the blood was human, but the forensic lab did more extensive tests and was able to come up with the blood type. Which has just told us that the blood isn't Celeste Perry's."

"So it was from one of the men," Chloe concluded.

"We have Celeste's pre-1960 medical records to let us know if it matched hers. We don't have anything on either of the men, but by process of elimination, since it's definitely not Celeste's blood, it's certainly a possibility that it's one of theirs. Luke and the rest of the cops here are going over the old investigation. Now that my tests have been confirmed, and the pathologist has found hair and tissue, too, there might need to be a search for a body."

"Wow, big goings-on in Northbridge."

"Yeah, everybody's been talking about it," Reid said.

"Don't you need to let your brother or someone else on the police force know what you just found out?"

"Forensics is calling Luke with the formal report. The call to me was more courtesy because I went to med school with the pathologist," Reid said just as the doorbell rang.

He pushed off the door, turned and opened it, greeting a teenager by name. Chloe didn't recognize either the teenager or the name—a testament to how long she'd been away from Northbridge.

When Reid had paid for the pizza, he closed the door and finally joined her on the floor with the large box safely between them.

Paper plates, napkins and prewrapped packets of plastic cutlery had also been delivered and Reid divided them evenly before opening the box to reveal a pizza identical to what they'd shared numerous times in the past.

"It doesn't look as if it's changed," Chloe commented, breathing deeply of the aroma of Paul's special blend of spices and seasonings.

"You know Northbridge—not too much does."

Reid served her a slice and then took one for himself, biting into its tip while Chloe used fork and knife. She pronounced it as good as ever after her first taste.

But with the renewed town scandal update exhausted and the subject of their dinner explored as far as it could be, an awkward silence fell. And since Reid had carried the conversation to that point, Chloe felt obligated to make her own contribution.

She just couldn't think of what to say and settled on small talk that she knew he probably wasn't interested in. But anything was better than the silence, so she glanced at the progress he'd made painting the room and said, "It looks like you got more done than I did today. I spent all afternoon arguing with the company I rented the car from."

"They weren't happy about the accident," Reid guessed.

"That wasn't the worst of it. I took out the insurance but they lost the paperwork and were trying to claim that I wasn't covered. I had to go through channels to get them to acknowledge that I was, but even then they wanted me to pay to have the car towed back to Billings. I had to fight to get them to agree to do it themselves and then—for the third round—I had to force them to honor the clause in the contract that says they'll send out a replacement."

"Are they going to?"

"Reluctantly, since I'm 'in the middle of nowhere' as they said. But they won't get one out here until the end of the week—Friday or Saturday. They insist that they can't do it before then and nothing I said—or threatened—made any difference. They were big jerks."

Something about her rant made Reid smile slightly and for no reason Chloe understood, the entire two hours of turmoil suddenly seemed worth it just to see that.

"I'll be around all week so if you need to go any-where that you don't feel like walking to, I can take you."

That offer was the second surprise of the evening and even though Chloe knew it probably wouldn't be smart to take him up on it unless she had to, it pleased her to have it on the table.

"Thanks," she said simply.

She turned down a second piece of pizza but Reid helped himself to another slice and said, "So. What do you do for a living?"

More safe, surface chat. But Chloe was grateful for it.

"You know the toy prizes in kids' meals at fast-food restaurants? I design them."

Another smile that sent a little warmth all through her.

"You're kidding," he said.

"Nope, I'm not kidding. Movie tie-ins. Spinning things. Wheelie things. Dolls. Action figures. Magic tricks. You name it, I've done it."

"How did you get into that?"

"I kept up with the painting and drawing I'd always liked to do when I went to college. I thought I wanted to be a graphic artist. Designing a toy was an assignment in one of my classes and not only did I discover that I had a knack for it and enjoyed it, but the toy I designed—a robotic ladybug—ended up winning a couple of awards and being bought by a miniature toy company. Well, the company isn't miniature, only the toys are. Anyway, they offered me a job on the spot. I turned it down because I wanted to finish school, but they were still interested when I did. I've been with them ever since."

"Amazing."

He did seem amazed. And impressed. Although Chloe didn't know how impressive what she did was compared to what he did.

"How about you?" she countered. "You never said anything about wanting to be a doctor."

"That came out in college. About the same time I was

finding that I had an aptitude for the science classes I was also working for most of my tuition as a janitor at the hospital. Old Doc Seymour noticed that I was interested and encouraged me—actually he took me under his wing and taught me a lot before I even got into med school. He also put in a good word for me when it came time to apply and that didn't do any harm in getting me in."

"Where did you go?"

"Wayne State, in Detroit. I did my residency there, too. In the heart of the city. After that, coming back to Northbridge was a day in the park."

"It can't be too much of a day in the park if you're the only doctor here," she said, recalling his comment from that morning about needing a replacement to cover his vacation.

"It's time consuming," he admitted. "And tough getting enough sleep now and then. But I have it better than old Doc Seymour who did it before me because now there's more supplementary staff—besides three nurses to Doc Seymour's one, I have a nurse-practitioner and a physician's assistant, too, which helps."

"And what happened to old Doc Seymour?" Chloe asked but with some hesitancy, because talking about Northbridge's former doctor took them closer to their past than she wanted to venture.

"He did what he always said he was going to do— he retired to his cabin out by the river and fishes a lot."

"He doesn't practice medicine anymore at all?"

"He comes into the hospital every Wednesday, walks around, pokes his nose in here and there, wants to know about any new *gadget* I'm using. But he's eighty-six now, his eyesight isn't great and if I'm seeing one of his former patients he likes to sit in. Sometimes even with lousy vision he still picks up on things I miss."

"Do you like being a doctor?"

"Yeah, especially here. I get to do a little of everything and sort of take over the surrogate dad role old Doc Seymour played—even though I'm too young for it," he added with a laugh.

Reid as a dad—surrogate or otherwise. Not a subject she wanted to get anywhere near.

As if he'd thought the same thing after making that comment, he glanced at his watch and said, "I should go."

Chloe didn't dispute it. But she did say, "No more pizza?" And she said it with a touch too much hopefulness in her tone.

"I think I've had my limit," he answered, closing the lid on the box. "Besides, the leftovers will give you something to eat around here. Didn't you always claim that was your favorite breakfast?"

"Mmm, cold pizza—it's a treat," she confirmed.

He got to his feet then and so did she, keeping her distance as he put on his coat. But she did follow behind as he headed for the door so she could lock it after him.

He didn't go out, though. He stopped there, and with one hand on the knob, he met her gaze.

"This was okay," he seemed to conclude.

Not an accolade but under the circumstances Chloe took it as high praise.

"It *was* okay," she agreed.

"So do you think we can do this? Let bygones be bygones or something?"

"What do you think?" she asked. "I mean, do you think you can let bygones be bygones? Or something?"

He studied her for a long moment with those brilliant green eyes. And while they still didn't look at her the way they had fourteen years ago, they also didn't look at her the way they had the night before or that morning. And that was a relief. Even if she *did* still yearn a little for more.

"I can give it a try," he said when he finally did answer.

"I'd like that," Chloe responded quietly.

"I guess I'll see you tomorrow then. How early can I start without disturbing you?"

"Anytime. Just use the key Betty gave you and come in. Even if it's before I'm awake I can't hear much of anything upstairs and I'll probably sleep through it."

"Okay, but I'll be especially quiet until I know you're up."

She nodded.

"Good night, then."

"Get home safely," she joked, making him smile a little again.

For another moment they remained standing there, not too far apart, just looking at each other.

As they did, Chloe couldn't help recalling so many other times when they'd said good-night at her door much like that. Only then he would have kissed her.

He would have kissed her in a way that would have filled her with a special kind of heat. That would have made her feel like his and his alone...

And of course that didn't happen tonight.

Instead Reid broke the glance first, looking at the handle as he turned it to open the door.

"Thanks for the pizza," she said belatedly.

"Sure," he answered as he went out into the clear autumn night.

Then he closed the door behind him and Chloe stepped up to lock it.

When she did she could feel the warmth of his hand lingering on the knob and all on their own her eyes closed and she absorbed that sensation, picturing those other nights, those kisses that had sent her to bed with a smile on her face.

Those kisses…

She couldn't help wondering if those kisses were anything like Reid's kisses now. Or if, as had happened with his looks, his kisses had changed and matured, too.

And even though it was completely uncalled for, even though it was its own kind of torture for her, she also couldn't help—in a secret, forbidden place deep inside of her—wishing she'd gotten a taste of his kiss, old or new, tonight.

Chapter Four

"Don't get scared—I'm coming up."

Chloe heard Reid's warning from the bottom of the stairs to the attic. The sound of his deep voice and the thought that he was on his way to see her were enough to make her pulse race.

There was nothing she could do to slow her heartbeat; she just tried not to pay attention to it. Or to the fact that it meant she was glad he was coming to see her.

It was after seven o'clock Tuesday evening and although they'd both been in the house all day, they hadn't actually connected. Chloe had been awake, lying in bed when she'd heard the front door open at 8:00 a.m. Moments later she'd also heard Reid climb the steps to the second floor, stop just outside of her bedroom door and then go back downstairs, leaving the scent of fresh coffee to drift in to her.

Curiosity had prompted her to get up and peek out the bedroom door where she'd found a foam cup full of wake-up-call waiting just outside.

She'd called a "Thank you!" in Reid's wake, he'd hollered back, "You're welcome," and that was that. They hadn't set eyes on each other.

Since coffee was frequently all she had for breakfast, she'd decided to skip the cold pizza and merely make the hot beverage her meal. Sipping it after she'd showered and dressed for the day, she'd gone directly to the attic.

When she'd stopped for lunch and finally trespassed into Reid's territory downstairs, he'd been on his cell phone, apparently discussing a medical case. So Chloe had merely waved to him, snatched a slice of the cold pizza and a soda from the fridge and returned to the attic to eat while she attempted to put some sort of order to what she needed to do there.

Which was where she was and what she was doing still when he appeared in the doorway at that moment.

"Hi," she greeted, slipping her hair behind her ears as she glanced up from the small stool where she was sitting in the middle of the attic floor.

"Hi to you, too," he responded. "You've been up here so long without even poking your nose out that I was beginning to wonder if I should check and see if a giant attic rat had taken you prisoner."

Chloe laughed and wrinkled her nose at the same time. "A giant attic rat? There better not be any rats up here, giant or otherwise."

Reid came all the way into the attic, stopping not far from where she was and surveying the room.

As he did, she surveyed him. He was dressed almost exactly as he had been the day before—jeans and a white crewneck T-shirt, both of them similarly paint-stained. But unlike the previous evening, tonight his face was cleanly shaven, as if he'd left when the five o'clock shadow had appeared to remove it before coming back. Before climbing the steps to her.

Chloe liked the look of him both ways—scruffy and clean-shaven—but it gave her a bit of satisfaction to think that tonight he'd cared enough to do the second shave.

After a moment of studying the attic he said, "I was kind of surprised when we toured the house and saw how much stuff was up here."

"Me, too. Apparently moving in a hurry leaves a lot behind."

"It's cleaner than it was when I initially saw it, but after all the hours you've put in, I thought you might have made a dent."

"Yesterday was cleaning day—dust and cobweb duty. Today I've just been trying to get some idea of what I'm dealing with and how to organize it. Once I'd cleared some spaces for what will need to be thrown out, what can go to charity and what I'll take with me piles, I barely got started actually going through anything. Hopefully I'll make more headway tomorrow."

"Big job."

"Bigger than I'd anticipated," Chloe said.

She debated about whether to say what was next on her mind, wondering if it would be a sore subject for

Reid. But then she decided that she'd merely been enjoying what she'd been doing for the last half hour and if it didn't bother her, maybe it wouldn't bother him either.

So she said, "I started with some of my own stuff—" She pointed at two boxes set to one side. "Those are just old clothes and things I'll donate to the church. But this box might interest you." She nodded at the cardboard storage box at her feet, decorated with heart and flower stickers, and with Private! written in several places in bright pink marker.

"I don't know," he said, playing along. "It says it's private."

"To keep my parents out of it if they came across it hidden under my bed. But there are some things in it that you might even want back."

"You found things of mine?"

"Mementos and keepsakes of dates," she confided. Then she altered her tone and said, "Unless you'd rather not…"

Reid glanced into the box as cautiously as if something might jump out at him, and Chloe had the impression he was using that brief time to consider whether or not he did want to take that stroll down memory lane.

Then, as if his curiosity had gotten the best of him, much as it had her over coffee that morning, he said, "A hamburger wrapper?"

Chloe took it out of the box and handed it to him. "From Tastee Dog. It was where you took me to dinner before the Homecoming dance my freshman year. Is it still open?"

"Tastee Dog? Thriving. Being across from the school keeps it going."

He studied what he was holding in hands that seemed bigger to Chloe than they had been fourteen years ago and she wondered if that was possible.

Then he said, "You honestly kept an old hamburger wrapper?"

"I not only kept it, I washed it, ironed it and had it taped to my wall for a while. That was not only my first date with you, it was my first date *ever* and I had to beg and bargain to get my parents to let me go. After all, you know how my parents were and I was only fourteen and you were the big man on campus at fifteen."

Reid gave the hamburger wrapper back to her, rolled his eyes and, as if he were a pre-adolescent boy, said, "Girls are so sappy."

"Be careful, there are a couple of things in here that were pretty sentimental and sappy of you."

"Nah, never happened," he joked. "I'm a tough guy."

"Oh, Tough Guy, you're just asking for it," Chloe countered, searching through the box until she found what she was looking for.

"An old milk bottle and a broken arrow—were you going through my trash or what?" he said as if he'd never seen them before.

Chloe playfully swatted his shin with the back of her hand. "You *gave* them to me and I know you remember."

He must have been drawn in in spite of himself because he sat down then, with the side of one thigh pressed to the floor and his other leg bent at the knee to brace his arm. He was also smiling a Cheshire cat smile that told her he *did* remember whether he wanted to admit it or not.

But just to bring home her point, she said, "It was from *our* song, the one that was playing on the radio when you said we were together—the Rod Stewart love song. This is a bottle of rain—evaporated now, but it was a bottle of rain—and this is a broken arrow."

"It's a good thing that was a wet spring or I still might not have that bottle filled," he said by way of admission. "I'd leave it out every time it was supposed to rain and one of my brothers would get to it before me and dump it just to be ornery. I finally had to put it on the roof after they were all asleep one night and get up before any of them did the next morning."

"So it would really be a bottle of rain and not just a bottle of water—I thought it was the most romantic thing anyone would ever do for me," Chloe confessed.

"And was it?"

"Pretty much," she said with a laugh.

Then, to avoid dwelling on that, she took out a shoe box and lifted the lid to show him what appeared to be a collection of scraps.

"Stubs," she dubbed it all. "Well, stubs and receipts and matchbooks and napkins and any little thing I could put in my purse as a souvenir of almost every place we ever went."

"Kleptomania?"

"A teenage girl's need to immortalize everything that goes on with her boyfriend."

When Chloe closed the lid on the shoe box Reid peered into the larger storage box again. "I see a whole bunch of dead flowers in there. What did they *immortalize?*"

"Some are flowers you gave me on birthdays or special occasions or just to be sweet, and the rest are corsages from every dance we went to—ten all together."

"Did we go to ten dances?"

"That Homecoming dance my freshman year was our first date—you were a sophomore. We went to that, the Christmas dance and the Pre-Spring Fling that year—we couldn't go to the prom because we were too young. That's three dances. My sophomore year—your junior—we went to all four dances. That makes seven. And the year you were a senior we missed only the Pre-Spring Fling. A total of ten."

"You had the flu the night of the Pre-Spring Fling," Reid contributed.

Chloe scrounged in the box again and as she did she said, "And you came over and sat with me the whole night anyway and brought me Spiderman comic books." When she found the old issues she took them out to show him she'd kept them, too.

"I brought you compelling literature and you just fell asleep on me."

Literally—she'd fallen asleep with her head on a pillow in his lap while he'd stroked her hair.

"And you didn't want to wake me so you stayed until I woke up on my own and missed your curfew and got into trouble," Chloe finished.

He shrugged a broad shoulder. "It was no big deal."

"It was a big deal to me. You know I wouldn't have

dared come home late or it would have been the last time I ever got to see you."

Reid didn't comment on that but instead glanced into the box once more, taking out a flyer printed on green paper. "Raleigh Sings Requests!" he read, his tone as excited as if he'd made a great discovery. "You actually kept this?"

"How else were you going to track down Raleigh so we could have him sing at our wedding?" Chloe asked, referring to a running joke they'd had.

They'd both belonged to the school choir and during Reid's senior year there had been a three-day concert they were invited to perform at in Billings. By then several of their friends had coupled up, too, and on the last night of the trip, wanting a date in the bigger city, Chloe and Reid and four other young lovebirds had snuck out of their hotel rooms after lights-out and gone to the only place they could get to—the hotel lounge that featured the entertainment of Raleigh Riley, who claimed to be able to sing any song requested of him. Raleigh had been an eighty-year-old man with an acoustic guitar, a reedy voice and a five-song repetoire.

"We had fun that night," Reid reminisced. "In spite of Raleigh's bad singing.

"Raleigh's bad singing of bad songs," Chloe added as they laughed again and ignored the part about those early, innocent dreams of the marriage they'd been so sure they would have in the future.

"Here are your waders," Chloe said then, producing the rubber fishing gear. "I thought you might want them back."

"Ah, I made you wear them for the car wash to raise money for the choir trip," Reid recalled.

"So I wouldn't get wet."

His grin was wily. "Actually it was so you wouldn't wear those short, short cutoffs. I was protecting what was mine."

Chloe had known that that was his motive, she'd just repeated what he'd claimed all those years ago. But his adolescent possessiveness had seemed endearing then and for some reason it gave her a little rush again now.

And even though she'd known what he was doing all along, she pretended this was news to her. "You were ugly-fying me?"

"I had to. I knew at least three guys who would have never been able to concentrate on soapy sponges if I hadn't."

"Ah, it was for the greater good."

"Exactly."

The last thing in the box was an old flannel shirt that had been Reid's. Chloe had conned him out of it so she could have something of his to wear. Something that would touch her bare skin and remind her of him when she wasn't with him.

It suddenly occurred to her that it was also something she didn't want to part with even now.

But still she took it out and handed it to him. "You probably want this back, too, even though it would look better on me."

The sight of the shirt made Reid smile a different kind of smile. A secret, pleased sort of smile.

"I used to love seeing you in that," he said then.

For a moment neither of them said anything else. They merely looked at the shirt. And maybe a little back in time, too. To when simply being together, sharing any food, any experience, sharing anything at all, made it special.

Then Reid folded the shirt and gave it to Chloe. "You keep it," he said, but not as if he didn't want it because it held bad memories. It was more as if he genuinely wanted her to have it.

And Chloe accepted it the same way, because she *did* want it. And because that contemplative moment had, for the first time since she'd returned to Northbridge, made Chloe feel a semblance of closeness to him again.

But before things became awkward she rifled through the box once more and then said, "I think that's it."

"No pictures?" he said as if that fact disappointed him. "Seems like we had a lot of them taken of us along the way. I even have a few and I didn't wash, iron and keep hamburger wrappers."

Chloe had more than a few old photographs. She had an entire album of snapshots of the two of them, and some of only Reid that she'd taken herself. But she wasn't going to tell him about the quantity. Or the fact that even now she knew exactly where in her apartment that album was, or that she still took it out periodically to look through it.

Instead she said, "I managed to hide the pictures to take with me so there aren't any left here."

"You had to *hide* them?"

"You know how it was. My parents—especially my mother—wanted every sign that you and I had ever known each other wiped away. I was surprised when I found this box. She tore my room apart when everyone was gone that last night after…things fell apart…and ordered my father to burn anything that had anything to do with you so I couldn't take a single reminder to my grandparents' house. The pictures were underneath some clothes so she missed them. My father must have stashed this without my mother knowing."

That sobered Reid and brought an instant frown to his handsome face. Chloe understood it. She was just sorry to see it. Sorry to have damaged the mood.

Reid seemed to shake it off a moment later but their journey backward was effectively ended so Chloe put the lid back on the storage box and their past together, and said, "Are you finished working for the day?"

Reid didn't resist the change of subject. "Finished for the day and finished painting the living room. I thought I'd come up here and make you stop, too, so after I change clothes I can take you over to the store to do some grocery shopping. You can't live on a cup of coffee and a slice of pizza. You need some supplies."

Chloe made a face. Of course she knew she needed to stock the fridge a little—and replace the Walkers' sodas—and she'd fully intended to make one trip to the grocery store. It was just that now that actually venturing into the Northbridge community was upon her, she wasn't eager to do it.

"Isn't it too late to grocery shop around here?" she said, hedging.

"The Groceries and Sundries started staying open a few nights a week while the college is in session because they were losing business to the convenience store."

So much for that dodge.

"You've been working since early this morning, you can't want to do that now," she tried.

Reid stared at her, studying her.

Then he said, "It's not a problem for me. Is it a problem for you?"

Not the problem he thought it was. Chloe could tell he thought she was dragging her feet because she didn't want to be with him. And while that *should* have been the case, it wasn't. In fact, being with him had much too much appeal.

She didn't want him to know that, but she also didn't want things between them to deteriorate again because he believed the opposite.

So she said, "I'll be honest with you, I'm not wild about the idea of making much of an appearance in Northbridge. I was hoping I'd hit town, make one stop at the store for staples, then dig in here, do what I needed to do and get out again with minimal exposure. But the storm and the accident messed up those plans and I seem to be turning into more of a coward the longer I'm here."

"What are you afraid of?"

"I don't know," she said. "It's probably silly after all this time, but I know how this town is and I'm sure *the Carmichael girl* getting pregnant at seventeen was the topic of conversation for weeks after word got out."

"Sure," Reid confirmed. "That and your mother going into that tirade that night we all came to tell your folks. Throwing me and my mother and even the minister out of the house and drawing the attention of the neighbors—there was talk."

"And I know how my mother and her friends treated people who were involved in scandals—whispering, staring, noses in the air—"

Reid nodded. "But there's only a handful of people who did—who do—that. Plus it's been a long time, Chloe. I don't think that'll happen now. I mean, yes, word is already out that you're back, my mom had heard it by six this morning and called me to ask if it was true. But whatever it is that's going on with that old bank robbery and the reverend's wife is what's really whetting everybody's appetite at the moment. When it comes to you, people will just be looking forward to seeing you again, and wondering what's gone on with you in the past fourteen years. I guarantee there won't be any pointing or staring or whispering or noses in the air. Even if we do run into anybody from your mother's former circle of friends."

"I don't know…"

"Come on. You need to get out, breathe some fresh air, buy some groceries, see for yourself that there's nothing to be worried about. Nobody stoned me, why would they stone you?"

Chloe thought that so many years had passed since Reid had weathered the storm that he'd probably forgotten what it was like to face people for the first time. But for her, this would be the first time. And regardless of what the scandal main course was these days, she found it difficult to believe that she wouldn't be a sumptuous side dish.

In the silence left by her indecision, Reid said, "You know we weren't the first kids in that situation or the last. We really are ancient history around here."

He got to his feet then and held out a hand to her. "I'll prove it to you. If I'm wrong, I'll buy your groceries."

Chloe gave it more thought, factoring in Reid's reaction to her on Sunday night and coming to the conclusion that, after that, nothing could be as bad. Plus she *was* beginning to feel cooped up in the house, and she did need food.

"I'd have to change clothes," she warned.

"Me, too. But after we do your shopping I'll take you back to my house and feed you my mom's spicy Southwestern chicken casserole. She brought it over this morning, Luke is working tonight and I can't eat it all alone. It'll be your reward for facing your fears. Or your embarrassment or whatever you want to call it."

"I always did love that casserole."

"I know, you never could pass it up. Now come on, if it's too slow a night at the store they'll close anyway. We have to get going."

Chloe hesitated a minute more, hearing too many of her mother's harsh words in her head.

But she opted for trusting Reid and ignoring those long-ago predictions.

"Okay, but if you're wrong I'm buying gourmet groceries to run up a huge tab for you to pay."

"Deal," Reid agreed. "Now get a move on."

Without thinking, Chloe accepted the hand he was still holding out to her and let him help her up.

But as they turned off the lights and left the attic Chloe had completely forgotten her own reluctance to be seen in Northbridge again.

Because all she could think about was how it had felt to have her hand in Reid's hand again—big and warm and strong.

How terrific it had felt. How they had seemed to fit together as perfectly as they had as teenagers.

And how sorry she'd been when he'd let go....

Chapter Five

Chloe used the next half hour for a super-quick shower and shampoo before slipping into clean jeans and a yellow scoop-neck sweater over a white camisole tank top.

As she lightly applied makeup that included a touch of powder to brighten her complexion, blush to highlight her cheekbones, mascara to add some definition to her blue eyes and the finishing touch of a pale lipstick, she told herself she wasn't doing this for Reid. She was doing it merely to put her best foot—or face—forward in her initial foray into Northbridge, which might thrust her into contact with anyone who had known her in the past.

But as she brushed out her hair, twisted it up the back of her head to leave the ends in a wavy geyser at her crown, she knew that her late-day makeover had every bit as much to do with Reid as it did with anyone she might happen to encounter.

It was just that she realized she had to keep anything to do with him in check.

When it came to romantic relationships, Chloe was very clear on one thing—there was no going back. It was something she'd learned the hard way herself, that a romance that had ended once with hurt and resentment couldn't successfully flourish on a second go-round.

"Some things just don't disappear," she told her reflection in the mirror above the bathroom sink as if she needed it said out loud.

Things like hurt and anger and resentment were deep wounds. And even if those wounds healed, they still left scars. Permanent emotional scars that, in her experience, meant that nothing could ever truly be the same again. Regardless of how hard both people tried to make it the same again or to pretend that it was. There just wasn't any going back—especially not back fourteen years—and she needed to keep that in mind.

The best that she could hope for with Reid was that they might be able to move forward. Slowly forward. To what, she didn't know. To being friendly acquaintances, she guessed.

And it seemed as if they might have taken those initial steps, at least, so she knew she should be content with that.

"Forward, not backward," she ordered her reflection. "Never backward. You really can't go home again."

But that belief notwithstanding, when her doorbell

rang, and she knew Reid was downstairs waiting for her, she felt a sudden rush…just as she had when she was fourteen and he'd come to pick her up for their first date.

Two days of sunshine had melted the snow and without the blizzard conditions that had blocked her view on the way into Northbridge on Sunday night, Chloe could see that the town was already all dressed up for Halloween, even though it was weeks away. Reid drove the few blocks out of the neighborhood streets to Main Street. At the southernmost end of Main was the town square with the white octagonal gazebo at its center decorated with orange lights strung from the eaves of the red roof. Tiny white lights followed each of the eight points of that roof to the cupola where more orange lights were strung around that.

Orange and white lights also wrapped the banisters on both sides of the five steps that led to the gazebo, the trunks of the numerous trees in the square and each of the Victorian streetlight poles there, and all along Main Street itself. Bundles of dried cornstalks, pumpkins and gourds adorned the space between each streetlight along Main where the windows of the various quaint, old-fashioned buildings that housed businesses and shops held their own contributions in the form of scarecrows, warty-nosed witches, spiderwebs, skeletons and various other Halloween paraphernalia.

"I forgot that Northbridge goes all out decorating for holidays," Chloe told Reid as she drank in the sight to keep her focus on something other than him.

He'd showered and changed clothes, too. Chloe knew he'd showered because he smelled of soap and cologne, and he wore fresh jeans and a hunter-green Henley shirt over a white crew-necked T-shirt.

The fact that he looked and smelled good made remembering that they were embarking on that new, only-acquaintances relationship all the more difficult, but paying attention to the Halloween lights and decorations helped to diffuse some of the effects.

The Groceries and Sundries store was where it had always been—midway up Main Street near the town's only stoplight. Since there were two cars parked head-first in front of it, it appeared to still be open even though there weren't any people in sight—something that Chloe was glad of. The fewer people she had to face on this maiden outing, the better, as far as she was concerned.

"That's my brother Ad's place across the street," Reid informed her as he pulled into an empty parking spot.

Following the aim of the thumb he poked over his shoulder, Chloe glanced back at what had been the local not-particularly-well-kept bar when she'd lived in Northbridge before. But now the shabby wooden front had a brick facade and large windows with dark green café curtains halfway up. It looked as if it had been turned into an English pub below a neon sign that announced the establishment as Adz.

"Your brother bought the bar?" Chloe said as Reid cut the engine and removed the key from the ignition, and they both got out of the car.

"It's a restaurant and bar now, but yeah, he did. A few years ago when old man Marshall wanted out."

"It looks a lot nicer now," Chloe observed.

"It is. Ad does good business there, too," Reid added as they went into the store.

Because Northbridge was so compact there was a lot of walking to destinations rather than driving, and so the lack of cars out front didn't mean a lack of customers inside the Groceries and Sundries. It wasn't packed with people, but there were more of them inside than Chloe had anticipated and she braced for the disapproval and scorn her mother had convinced her she would be met with should she ever show her face in the small town again.

It didn't happen right off the bat, though. The first two shoppers she and Reid encountered weren't familiar to Chloe. The two girls seemed about college age and while Reid answered their greetings, they moved on before he had the chance to introduce her. But the third person they met was Mrs. Gloria Wilkie.

Chloe didn't know if it was still the case, but fourteen years ago Gloria Wilkie had been the president of the Ladies' Church League, a member of Chloe's mother's book club, and one of the biggest gossips the town had to offer. What Chloe *did* know was that Gloria Wilkie was about the last person she would have chosen to meet up with again. Ever.

Chloe stopped short when she saw the older woman and actually considered turning around and going the other way before the now gray-haired Mrs. Wilkie could look up from the canned goods and recognize her.

But considering retreat wasn't doing it and before Chloe had decided one way or another, the woman spotted her.

"Chloe Carmichael? Is that you?"

Reid must have known how Chloe felt because he grasped the back of one arm in a steadying hand, gave it a supportive squeeze and then let go. And remarkably, it helped.

"Yes, it's me. Hello, Mrs. Wilkie," Chloe responded.

The older woman raised her gaze to Reid and arched an eyebrow. "And with Reid Walker. Of course."

"Gloria," Reid said firmly, authoritatively, and almost with a sort of warning in his voice.

Which was when it occurred to Chloe that Reid was probably now the woman's doctor. It almost made her smile to think about. It also made it slightly easier to continue, although she wasn't sure why that should be the case.

Gloria Wilkie returned her closely spaced eyes to Chloe. "I'd heard you were in Northbridge again."

"Just for a little while to go through some things my parents left at the house," Chloe answered.

"I was sorry to learn about your parents' deaths."

"Thank you."

"I always thought highly of your mother. She was a decent, moral, upstanding woman, and an asset to this community while she was here."

Chloe wasn't sure if that was a jab at her personally, if Gloria Wilkie was letting her know she didn't count Chloe in that same category, but she decided the best route was to merely agree that her mother was, indeed, what Gloria Wilkie considered her to have been.

"Yes, she was," Chloe said simply enough.

"Had things been different, your mother would have made one of the best mayor's wives Northbridge ever had."

"I'm sure she would have," Chloe agreed again.

"We—her friends—considered it a travesty that she felt she couldn't stay here. But she told me personally that she was so mortified she just couldn't look everyone in the eye."

Chloe didn't think there was any doubt about it now—Gloria Wilkie was definitely taking stabs at her.

She chose not to respond to that one. But it didn't stop the woman from adding facetiously, "I certainly hope you at least made something of yourself."

"She designs toys," Reid contributed before Chloe could. "Award-winning toys."

"Just one award, early on," Chloe amended even though she appreciated Reid's subtle accolade in response to the other woman's unsubtle attack.

"Well, isn't that good for you," the older woman said as if it wasn't at all. "I hope that made your mother's sacrifice worth it."

Reid sighed loudly enough and disgustedly enough to be heard. Then he took a look into the handbasket Gloria Wilkie was carrying and said, "Looks to me like you should be paying some attention to your own business, Gloria. What did I tell you about the red meat? You swore you were hardly ever eating it. I believe you said something about how diligent and dedicated to

your health you were being and that temptation was
nothing to you. Unlike other people. But I see two big,
juicy steaks there. Apparently even you make mistakes
sometimes."

"Apparently. But my mistakes only harm me,"
Gloria Wilkie countered, clearly miffed with the local
doctor and tossing one of her barbs in his direction.
Then, as if the fun had gone out of the moment for her,
she said, "I'd better get home to Bill—he'll be wondering where I am. Again, Chloe, my condolences."

Chloe merely raised her chin in acknowledgment
before the woman walked in the other direction and left
her alone on the aisle with Reid.

He leaned close to her ear and whispered, "Okay, so
maybe there will be a few stones thrown. But you know
Gloria Wilkie is the worst and now that's over with."

"Easy for you to say."

"I honestly didn't think you'd run into that kind of
thing after so long. I mean, I went through a whole lot
of shame-on-you's at the time, but—"

"You did?"

"Hey, it's Northbridge, where everyone feels free to
reprimand everyone else's kid if the kid gets out of
line. Plus I didn't have a father, remember? A whole
slew of helpful souls felt inclined to call me on the
carpet for putting my poor mother through more than
she'd already been through with my dad dying and her
being left with five kids to raise on her own. But I
honestly didn't think anyone would bring it up now."

Chagrined by the reminder that Reid had had to face
the music on his own while she'd just had his help and

support, Chloe couldn't be upset with him for miscalculating what the response to her might be. So rather than saying I-told-you-so, she said, "No one is nastier than Gloria Wilkie, so hopefully you're right and the worst is over."

That did prove to be true; as they progressed through the store they met three more people who recognized Chloe and all of them did exactly what Reid had predicted before—they were pleasant, pleased to see her again, asked perfectly civil and courteous questions about where she was living now and what she was doing and said they hoped to see her again, particularly at the football game the next night.

Still, Chloe wasn't sorry to finish her shopping—at Reid's expense since he'd lost the bet that no one would say anything about their past—and get back to what seemed like safer territory.

Chloe's and Reid's first stop after grocery shopping was Chloe's house to put things away. Then they went across the street to the house Reid shared with his brother.

"I'm guessing you'll have a beer tonight," Reid said after he'd shown her around the small ranch-style two-bedroom home that was furnished carelessly enough to make it obvious two style-clueless men lived in it.

"You guess right," Chloe confirmed. "I will have a beer tonight."

He'd given her the task of setting the kitchen table with mismatched plates and silverware while he retrieved the casserole from the oven.

Chloe did that and then sat at the antiquated table she remembered being in his mother's basement years ago.

Before joining her, he took two beers from the old, squat fridge that he towered above, and opened them.

"Out of a glass or out of the bottle?" he asked then.

She hated to see what kind of glasses he had so she said, "The bottle is fine," and accepted one of the two he brought with him, tasting the dark ale before setting it on the table.

The casserole was a gooey blend of chicken, corn tortillas, tomatillo sauce, green chiles, sour cream, onions, pepper jack and cheddar cheeses. Reid served her more than she ever would have served herself, more than she thought she could eat, before spooning out some for himself and sitting across the table from her.

"So you left here for Arizona and stayed there, huh?" he said as they began to eat, obviously referring back to the question she'd answered three times tonight and on her medical forms on Sunday. "Over the years, I've wondered."

So, he *had* thought about her over the years....

Had all the thoughts been negative? Or, every now and then, had he recalled something good?

She hoped so.

But she didn't ask. She merely answered his question.

"You know my grandparents on my father's side were in Tucson—that's how my parents chose it in the first place. My dad could go right to work at his father's insurance agency and not lose any income since the whole move was done on the spur of the moment. Once we were there and he was doing that, my parents decided to stay."

"What about your dad's political aspirations? I wondered if someday I'd hear that he'd become mayor or governor of someplace, but I never did."

"Like everything else, politics in the city is on a much bigger scale than in a small town. Around here running for mayor just meant throwing a hat into the ring at a town council meeting. It meant talking to most all the voters personally in the course of a week or two, ordering a few signs and posters and some handout flyers that my folks would have been able to pay for because not that many would have been necessary. It meant probably hanging the signs and posters themselves, passing around the flyers or asking for them to be put in shop windows—"

"I'd never thought about it, but that *is* what gets done in the way of campaigning when we have an election."

"But in Tucson there needed to be financial backing. Affiliation with a party was preferable. There needed to be support from a lot of different people and organizations and newspapers and—" Chloe shrugged. "Like I said, a much bigger scale. He just never made it even to the point of getting enough backing to run for anything except city council and he lost those elections all four times he ran. He finally settled for taking over my grandfather's insurance agency when my grandfather retired."

"And did we get the blame?" Reid asked with an edge of anger to his voice.

Chloe smiled a rueful smile. "Not we. Me. My mother said it was my fault that we'd had to leave the one place where my father could have been mayor and had a political career."

"I can't imagine my mom laying that kind of thing on me," Reid said, taking a second helping of the casserole while Chloe neared finishing hers.

"My mother—and father—were definitely nothing like your mom," Chloe said. "If anything, they were a lot more like Gloria Wilkie."

A lot more.

Chloe's parents had been extremely strict and straightlaced. They'd been overly concerned with appearances and living up to sometimes ridiculously high standards.

And if Chloe didn't meet their standards—if the daughter they were determined would reflect well on them didn't—the tiniest infraction had, in her mother's estimation, been a catastrophe that she was convinced would have far-reaching consequences.

"I had to come to grips a long time ago with the fact that my parents—particularly my mother, who was the most outspoken of the two of them—just were the way they were. They loved me. They gave me everything I needed. They weren't abusive. But they weren't warm and fuzzy folks. There was no hugging in my house, that's for sure."

"No, I wouldn't call your parents warm and fuzzy," Reid agreed.

Of course he'd seen the worst of them, so he had no illusions.

"You don't get to pick your parents, you know," Chloe said. "You just have to deal with what you get and I got parents who—" she shrugged. "Who put a lot of pressure on me. Maybe because I was an only child. They expected a lot. They had a lot of rules—"

"And they came down too hard on you when you broke any of them—not that you did that anywhere near as many times as the rest of us."

Chloe laughed a little. "Like that fit my mother threw because she caught us holding hands at a *church* picnic—"

"I couldn't see you for a month after that."

"Two months the one time I forgot to take out the trash," Chloe reminded.

"And that was even *after* I raked all their leaves trying to get them to lighten up on you so we could go on the hayrack ride."

"Which I still didn't get to go on," Chloe finished, preferring to reminisce nostalgically than to recall her mother's raving and slamming of doors and predictions of a wretched future for anyone as inconsiderate and irresponsible as she was….

"Anyway," Chloe said then, "my father did fine in the insurance business. And he was president of a whole bunch of organizations connected with that. My mother got into charity and committee work and chaired most of those groups, so their lives were a long way from being destroyed."

"Unlike some," Reid muttered, the expression on his chiseled face hardening suddenly.

Chloe had no idea why or what he was referring to

since, as far as she could tell, neither of their lives had been destroyed by the events of fourteen years ago any more than her parents' lives had been.

But she didn't want to disturb the tentative peace they'd reached prior to that, so she pretended she hadn't heard what he'd said and instead she pushed her now-empty plate away and returned to a neutral topic. "Tell your mom thanks for the dinner, it was as fabulous as I remembered it being."

Reid nodded but he didn't say anything. He didn't even look at her. He just stared daggers at the beer bottle he had in the fierce grip of one hand. And even though she still didn't understand his change in attitude or his last comment, she could tell he was working to control his temper. Given that, the best course seemed to be to leave him to it.

He'd pushed his own plate away, too, so Chloe stood and took both hers and his to the sink to rinse them. It wasn't until she'd done that and was putting them into the dishwasher that Reid seemed to succeed at whatever it was he'd been struggling with and brought the casserole dish to the sink, too.

But he *had* calmed down again because in a semi-teasing tone, he said, "I can't believe you ate everything I put on your plate."

Chloe laughed, relieved that animosity wasn't going to poke its ugly head out again and damage this evening that she was enjoying more than she should be.

"I can't believe I ate so much either," she said. "I'm stuffed, but I love your mom's cooking and I just couldn't stop."

"Good thing you have a long walk home," he joked.

"And that's probably where I should be headed—it's been a long day for both of us and I imagine you're going to start early tomorrow morning again."

"Same time, same place," he confirmed.

Chloe noted that he hadn't tried to persuade her to stay longer. Taking that to mean he was ready for the evening to end, she went from the kitchen into the living room to put on the jacket she'd worn tonight.

"I'll go over with you. I want to check the last wall I painted today and make sure it doesn't need another coat. I don't think it does, but *if* it does, I'll have to do that before I start in the kitchen."

"Okay," Chloe said, wishing he was walking her home for another reason but happy to find that she would have even a few more minutes with him anyway.

"No jacket for you?" she asked when he opened the door and waited for her to go out ahead of him.

"I told you—I'm a tough guy."

"Oh, right, I forgot," she said with a laugh as they stepped into the cool evening air.

He let her unlock her own front door when they reached it, and in they went, greeted by paint fumes that luckily didn't invade the upstairs.

"What do you think?" Chloe asked after Reid had turned on the bare-bulbed lamp that was the only option in the room and checked his paint job.

"I think it's okay," he answered simply. Then, pointing to the lamp he was still standing near, he said, "On or off?"

"I don't need it on, I'm going right upstairs."

He switched off the light and returned to the door.

Chloe followed, again in order to lock up after him.

But she thought he was going all the way out and when he paused there instead, she nearly collided with him, stopping a bit closer than she would have otherwise.

Close enough to smell the faint scent of his soap and maybe his shampoo, and to see all too clearly the lines and angles of his drop-dead gorgeous face in the golden glow of moonlight and porchlight coming in through the open front door.

"So," he said, giving no indication as to whether or not he was aware of the fact that she was a tad too near. "Now that you've weathered the worst in Gloria Wilkie and have seen for yourself that other people aren't going to be as bitchy as she is, maybe you'd like to get out a little more. Tomorrow night is the first football game for the Bruisers—"

"The Bruisers?"

"Oh, right, that started after you'd moved. It's just a bunch of us local guys. We get together to play football or basketball or baseball, depending on the season. Mostly we play against each other unless the college kids come up with a group big enough to play against us. But tomorrow night will be just Bruiser against Bruiser. There's usually a big turnout, though—you know how it is around here, not many entertainments, so whenever anything does go on, most of the town shows up. And then, after the game, we're all going to Adz for the kickoff party." Reid shrugged much as she had earlier. "It's fun. I think you'd have a good time."

"I wondered what football game everybody at the

store was referring to," she said to buy herself a moment while she tried to figure out if he was merely suggesting she attend or if he was asking her to go with him.

Since it didn't seem clear either way, she said, "Are you saying we could go together?"

"I guess I am," he said as if it was coming as somewhat of a surprise to him.

Thinking about that odd remark he'd made earlier and his brief change of temper, she said, "You'd be okay with that?"

He didn't respond immediately. Instead he looked down at her, studying her with those green eyes that seemed never to miss any detail, seeming to seriously consider only now whether or not he really would be okay with the two of them attending a social event together.

Then he smiled with only one side of his agile mouth. "Yeah, I think I'd be okay with it. I think I'd actually look forward to tomorrow night even more than I already am."

That sounded like a revelation and a very big admission. And in the spirit of that, Chloe admitted to herself that while she wasn't any more thrilled with the idea of seeing an even greater number of people in Northbridge and happening across another Mrs. Wilkie, she was too thrilled with the thought that Reid wanted her to go with him to decline.

"You all regretted not being at a high school big enough to have sports teams so you formed one of your own, huh?" she said as a segue.

"That's about it. It's good exercise, we enjoy it, it's become a big deal."

"I think I'd like to see you play," she said.

"You can't do that unless you come," he challenged.

"Guess I'll have to, then."

He nodded and smiled a smile that was bigger than the one before but still not a grin, still slightly contemplative and reserved as he continued looking at her as if he were cataloguing the changes time had made in her face.

Then, as if he approved of what he was seeing, that reserved smile broadened just a bit.

And there they were, facing each other, separated by less space than was probably wise, looking into each other's eyes, and it was impossible for Chloe not to think once again about all the good-night kisses that had come out of this same position. But she kept telling herself that no matter what had happened hundreds of times in the past—the distant past—it wasn't going to happen now and she should *stop* thinking about it.

Which wasn't easy to do when it seemed as if Reid was leaning in a little, as if he actually might be on the verge of kissing her after all....

And suddenly she wasn't sure how she felt about that.

But before she could decide, he backed off. He stood straighter than he'd been before and he stepped out the door, adding distance on top of it.

"See you tomorrow," he said then, his voice an octave deeper and not much more than a whisper in the night.

"Thanks again for dinner," Chloe said almost as softly.

Reid only raised his chin in acknowledgement of that, turned and left.

And just that quickly, watching him go, Chloe knew how she felt about the possibility that he could have been on the cusp of kissing her.

As surely as she knew that Reid had done the right thing *not* kissing her, she knew that she would have liked it if he had.

And heaven help her, not even reminding herself that kissing was not an option here, that it was a very bad idea that should never be acted upon, could change that fact.

Chapter Six

"You're cutting it a little close," Reid greeted his brother Wednesday evening.

Reid had just come into the living room with his sports bag and what he was about to put in it when Luke rushed into their house barely thirty minutes before the football game was scheduled to start.

"And you're looking too prettied-up to be heading out for a game," Luke countered, obviously noticing the fact that rather than Reid's usual pregame attire of sweats, he was wearing jeans and a shirt. Plus he'd showered and shaved even though he'd be showering again after the game and putting on what would be his third set of clothes for the day.

But Reid didn't explain himself, he merely threw a towel at his brother and set his sports bag on the sofa.

Luke caught the towel and threw it back.

But Luke *did* explain why he was so late getting home. "I'm buried at work with this whole reverend's wife and the bank robbery thing. I probably shouldn't have left for the game tonight at all."

"What's going on?" Reid asked as he rolled the towel into a log and stuffed it into his bag.

"Right now we're just trying to gather information and what we can of the paperwork from the old investigations."

"Investigation*s*—plural?"

"Oh, yeah, definitely plural. That's one of the problems. We're dealing with the local investigation—such as it was—what the state cops did, and what the FBI did."

"The local investigation wasn't done well?"

"In 1960 Northbridge's police department was one guy—Howard Fox. It wasn't until after the college was built in '63 that we became a bigger force. And at the time that the robbery went down, Howard Fox had just been diagnosed with lung cancer. He was sick, his head wasn't in the job, and beyond documenting some things in a few reports, most everything went into the hands of the state guys and the feds—mainly the feds, because bank robbery falls under their jurisdiction."

"Plus we're talking decades of time passing since then. I don't suppose that helps," Reid contributed.

"Exactly. Both the state guys and the feds who handled the investigations are all either retired or dead. Fox left the job here within weeks after the robbery and it took six months to find someone else—an out-of-towner no one knew. By the time that guy took over—someone named Mirabelle, who is also now deceased—the robbery was apparently history. The only mention of it in any of his papers was a notation about the feds contacting him, telling him to keep an eye out for Celeste. He doesn't say why, so we don't know if there was reason to believe she might come back here or if it was a just-in-case kind of thing. And that's all Mirabelle left—there's nothing about whether or not he questioned anyone around here to find out if Celeste *did* come back, or if she might have contacted anyone, nothing."

Luke took off his jacket and tossed it over the back of the armchair as he continued. "No one working now for the state or the feds has any memory of this case whatsoever. Nothing was computerized then, which means a long paper trail and a lot of files stuck in boxes and stashed in storage for who knows how long with no easy, quick way to get to them for anyone to look anything up for us."

"What about newspaper reports? Would they help at all?"

"There just aren't many. A small-town bank robbery and the small-town reverend's wife running off with the robbers didn't get much press outside of Northbridge— some, but not much. The Northbridge paper kept it going longer than anyone else, through the initial investigation, but when there weren't any immediate arrests, even the articles here stopped. There have been a few anniversaries of the robbery that inspired the local paper to do the story all over again, but never with any new information or anything that would be useful."

"So what are you doing besides wanting to pull your hair out in frustration?"

Luke laughed a humorless laugh. "We're going over what Fox did leave behind and I have requests in to the state police and the FBI to locate the old files. When those are dug up, copies of them will be sent here, and since a few of the officers and agents who handled everything are still alive, we've been promised contact information so we can try to talk to them in hopes that they remember something."

"Sounds like a mess."

"Times ten. And not an efficient way to investigate."

Reid paused in what he was doing—carefully packing his post-game clothes—to look at Luke. "What *do* you know?" he asked.

"You mean other than that the bank was robbed, Celeste Perry left town with one or both of the robbers and that their names were Frank Dorian and Mickey Rider?" Luke said facetiously.

"Yeah, other than that stuff that everyone knows because it's been in the paper every day since the duffel was found."

"We know that it looks like the blood on the duffel may be Mickey Rider's," Luke said with a weary sigh.

"That's something," Reid pointed out to encourage his brother. "How did you come to that conclusion?"

"It isn't a complete conclusion yet. We had some minimal background information on both robbers and managed to get through to someone in Rider's hometown—a small place near Boise, Idaho. We learned that his blood type and the type on the duffel are the same."

"But it isn't a *complete* conclusion because that blood type is the most common and if the other guy had it, too—"

"Yep. We still need the blood type of the other guy. If it's different, then what we have on the duffel is probably Rider's blood. If both Rider and Dorian had the same type, we're back to square one. And we're having a tough time finding out what Dorian's blood type was—or is—because he was from Detroit."

"Bigger city, harder to trace him. Especially after all these years," Reid guessed.

"You got it."

"Have you found out yet which of the robbers the reverend's wife was hot for?"

"Fox tried to figure that out—it was one of the things in his reports. The problem was that the two men were always together so whenever the reverend's wife was with them, she could have been with either of them—"

"I keep wondering how that came about at all—a reverend's wife out with a couple of drifters?"

"It was all part of the scandal at the time that she was hanging around with them. Apparently the story at the start was that she was ministering to them, trying to bring them into the fold for her husband. I'm not sure who circulated that fable—maybe it was the excuse the reverend's wife was giving him and he repeated it to save face. But Fox wrote that it was obvious right away that Celeste wasn't *ministering* or trying to bring

Dorian and Rider into the fold. She was in the bar, drinking and dancing and kicking up her heels right along with them, and everyone was talking about it in spite of the reverend's stoicism."

"And is that how he handled it? Stoically? He didn't go into the bar and drag her home?"

"Fox wrote that that was what everyone was expecting him to do, but he didn't. He just stuck with the ministering-recruiting story and kept a stiff upper lip. Common consensus was that he was hoping if she had a little time to party she'd get it out of her system and go back to being the good wife and mother. It just didn't work out that way."

"And she wasn't hanging on to one robber more than the other?"

"Things pointed to her being with Dorian."

"Really?" Reid said as his own suspicions rose.

"Yeah, I know. If Celeste Perry was in bed with Dorian and the blood on the duffel belongs to Rider it makes you wonder if the two lovebirds didn't dispose of the third guy so they could go off on their own with all the loot."

"Right," Reid confirmed.

"It's certainly a theory we're keeping in mind. But at this point we have very few pieces of the puzzle so everything is just a guess." Luke poked his chin in Reid's direction. "Now, you want to tell me how come you're all gussied up to get sweaty and dirty on a football field?"

"Gussied up?" Reid repeated with a laugh.

"I smell the cologne and you didn't put that on for me and the rest of the Bruisers."

"I took Chloe to the store last night and after a million people told her she should come to the game tonight, I thought I had to ask her if she wanted to go."

"Like it's against your will," Luke said sardonically. "Like I haven't seen you standing at the living room window looking over there a dozen times already in the last couple of days. Like I don't know that you've been getting up early, going for coffee and bringing two cups across the street every morning. Like I don't know that you're staying over there even when your work is finished. Like I thought you just ate double the casserole last night. Like I'm not seeing all the signs that you're thinking about her every minute and getting about as wrapped up in her as you were when the two of you were kids."

"I'd think with all the bank robbery investigating that you're doing you'd be too burned out when you come home to play detective with me."

"Yeah, well, figuring out what's going on with you doesn't take any skills. I just can't figure out if you've totally forgotten what went on fourteen years ago or what."

"I haven't forgotten," Reid said, more seriously now.

"Because if I'm not mistaken," Luke persisted, "when I thought I was a father and then wasn't, it was you telling me you understood what it was like to lose a child. My impression was that that was still something you were carrying around with you. That and the anger at the woman who had cost you that child. Is all that gone now?"

Reid was finished packing his sport bag and he zipped the top. But he did it with more force than it required.

"I don't know," he said without looking at his brother. Then he amended his answer. "No, it isn't all gone. But sometimes it fades to the background."

"When you're with her."

"Right."

"You told me that you could never forgive her."

"That's what I said."

"Are you thinking that that isn't the truth? That now that you're seeing her again, maybe you *can* forgive her?"

"I don't know," Reid repeated. "I guess I haven't thought about forgiving, I've just been working not to think about what happened at all."

"How's that going for you?"

"Not so well sometimes," Reid answered wryly, recalling his conversation with Chloe the previous night and how he hadn't been able to suppress his own feelings entirely when she'd said that no one's life had been destroyed.

"Have you talked about it? Found out what was going through her mind at the time? Why she did what she did? Or at least did what her parents wanted her to do without even telling you first?"

Reid shook his head. "No, we haven't gone near any of that. It's like the elephant in the corner that we're both pretending we don't see."

"Maybe you should pull the elephant into the center of the room and stop pretending," Luke suggested.

More and more Reid had been considering doing just that.

But yet again he said, "I don't know."

"Do you at least know that she's starting to get to you

again?" Luke challenged. "Because I think that's something you should keep your eyes open to."

"They're open," Reid insisted.

Luke nodded, showing nothing that let his brother know if he believed that or not.

But rather than pursuing it he glanced at his wristwatch and said, "Geez, I'm late. I have to change."

"Yeah, you'd better get a move on," Reid agreed.

He was glad for the time constraints that had ended his conversation with his brother, though.

Glad to have that conversation ended.

Because as he shrugged into his jacket and shouldered his sports bag he was thinking that dealing with that elephant in the corner was more daunting than Luke knew.

And Reid could only do it when he was ready.

"Chloe? It *is* you!"

It might have been fourteen years since Chloe had heard that voice but she recognized it instantly: Sugar Benson, Chloe's best friend from the day Chloe had arrived in Northbridge until the day she'd left.

Chloe was smiling before she even raised her gaze from the football field.

"Sugar!"

Chloe was sitting on the highest bleacher, alone and at a distance from the rest of the onlookers who had come out to watch the game. When Sugar Benson reached her, her old friend sat beside her and simultaneously pulled her into a huge hug.

"I couldn't believe it when I came into town tonight

and heard you were in Northbridge. Then I look up and here you are. What were you thinking not to get a hold of me the minute you hit the county line?"

"I was thinking that I didn't know if you'd *want* to see me after all this time," Chloe confessed, hugging her former best friend as hard as Sugar was hanging on to her.

"Wouldn't *want* to see you? Why in the world would I ever not want to see you?"

"It's just been so long…." And even after Chloe was out from under the constrictions of her parents, she hadn't contacted Sugar because the thought of touching base with anyone she'd left behind here had seemed so complicated. So painful.

"Time doesn't matter when it comes to friends," Sugar assured.

They let go of each other but Sugar threaded her arm through Chloe's even as she reared back enough to look at her.

"You're making me feel like a blimp!" Sugar decreed. "You just got better—you're beautiful and trim and dressed to beat the band, and here I am a farmer's wife with two kids and another one set for Christmas delivery."

Chloe laughed and ignored the *dressed to beat the band* comment that made her feel as if she'd overdone it in the pinstriped gray slacks and the cashmere turtleneck sweater she was wearing. "You look wonderful and I thought I felt something kick me. You must have married Hank the way you always said you would."

"I wasn't going to let him get away, that's for sure. We got married the day after high school graduation. I wanted to invite you—I wanted you to be my maid of honor—but when I asked Reid what he thought he said that no letter he'd sent had ever gotten a reply and if I called—"

"I wouldn't have even seen a letter or have been allowed to talk to you," Chloe said before her friend finished.

"But now here you are and I'm so happy!" Sugar gushed, her eyes misting and making Chloe's eyes well up, too.

With a crack in her voice, Sugar said, "I wondered if I'd ever talk to you again. Are you married? Do you have kids? Do you work?"

"No, no and yes," Chloe answered her old friend's questions in the order in which they'd been asked, going on to tell Sugar what she did for a living and that yes, she still lived in Tucson.

"You must be in Northbridge about your folks' house," Sugar said then. "I heard you were selling it to Reid and Luke—although I was shocked to find out that Reid would go anywhere near that place. And tonight? Someone said you came with Reid. To watch him play. Can that be?" Sugar ended with a voice full of hope.

"Yeah, I guess it can be," Chloe answered tentatively.

Sugar shivered suddenly and said, "This game is almost over and the guys will go into the school to use the showers before we all end up at Ad's place. Let's get out of the cold and wait inside."

Sugar stood, pulling Chloe with her, obviously not considering whether or not Chloe wanted to see the rest of the game. And while the game itself didn't interest her in the slightest, she had been enjoying the opportunity to watch Reid.

But she didn't want to deny her old friend, especially not with ogling Reid as the reason. So she let Sugar tug her across the schoolyard and into the much warmer building where the high school classes were held.

"So. You and Reid together again…" Sugar said the minute they were inside, her tone inviting confidence.

"Oh, no, I wouldn't say that. At least not *like* that," Chloe answered in a hurry. "We're… Well, nothing. I mean, he's working on the house, I'm cleaning out the attic. He just let me tag along tonight to give me something to do."

Or so she had decided after thinking about tonight the whole day as she'd worked, after wondering if this was supposed to be a date. She'd finally convinced herself that of course it wasn't.

"But he *did* let you tag along," Sugar said. "That's something. That's *really* something after the grudge he's been holding against you all this time."

"I know he was none-too-happy to see me Sunday night," Chloe said, assuming that had been an indication of the grudge.

"I'm sure," Sugar said. "It was really rough on him. The way things ended up. Not that it wasn't rough on you, too, I'm sure. But we don't want to talk about that," she added, smoothing a hand over her very round belly.

"I was a little surprised by just *how* mad he still was," Chloe said anyway.

"You can't blame him. He took it all hard. Your mother treating him the way she did that last night and then after you were gone the next day—gloating and lording it over him, and not having any say about what you did with the baby—those were bad enough. But I think he thought if he could get you to run off with him when he went after you that he could swallow the stuff your mother had said and even the loss of the baby. But when you wouldn't, when you told him what you did… Well, then the whole thing came together for him and nearly ate him alive."

The more Sugar said, the more confused Chloe became.

"What do you mean the way my mother treated Reid after I was gone and that he didn't have any say about the baby? No one had any say about the baby—"

Sugar smiled sympathetically. "It's okay. I thought at the time that I might have done the same thing you did."

"What did I do? I didn't do anything."

"Really, it's okay. I understand."

But Chloe didn't.

"Seriously, Sugar, what—"

The door they'd come through a few minutes before opened just then and in came the Bruisers and a number of spectators. Noise and voices and bodies filled the corridor.

Sugar again took over, announcing to Reid when he reached them that she was taking Chloe with her to Adz ahead of him so they could have more time to talk and catch up while he showered, that he could meet them there with the other guys.

Reid accepted that and Chloe couldn't very well say no.

She also couldn't find an opportunity to get Sugar to clarify any of what she had said because several more players' wives came along with them in Sugar's van.

And even after they arrived at Adz there wasn't the privacy Chloe needed to continue her conversation with her old friend.

But that didn't leave Chloe with any fewer questions.

It did, however, leave her wondering if, once she made it through the rest of the evening, she should pose those questions to Reid instead....

Chapter Seven

The kickoff party after the football game was a bois-
terous affair that to Chloe, seemed to go on and on.
Under other circumstances she would have thoroughly
enjoyed it. There were no Mrs. Wilkie incidents. Everyone there was near her own age, and it was more like a
class reunion than anything. Old friends and acquaintances were glad to see her. A lot of updating was done,
no one mentioned what had driven Chloe out of Northbridge fourteen years ago, and no one seemed to pass
any kind of judgment the way her mother had so con-
vincingly claimed they all would.

But still, after her conversation with Sugar at the
school, what had happened fourteen years ago was on
Chloe's mind to such an extent that it took the pleasure
out of the evening. Too many things didn't seem to

have explanations. Some of the things Sugar had said
and her attitude had started it, but once it had, Chloe
began to think more about the level of contempt she'd
discovered in Reid on Sunday night and that odd
remark he'd made at dinner the night before, too.

What did all of that mean?

It was as if she were missing something. She just
didn't know what. And the more she tried to figure it
out, the more her mind tracked back fourteen years.

A week before her last night in Northbridge she'd
realized her period was very late.

That was certainly something she couldn't very well
confide in her mother, so she and Sugar had talked their
parents into letting them take the bus into Billings for
a day of shopping. But the only item on their shopping
list had been a home pregnancy test that Chloe had
taken into the restroom of the store where she'd purchased it.

The test had been positive, the results proving her
worst fears. That one time—her first time—of making
love, when Reid had been housesitting for a mutual
neighbor, when they'd spent an evening alone there
while her parents were at a town meeting and didn't
know she was gone, had led her and Reid to get so carried away that not only had they made love, but they
hadn't used any protection. One time and Chloe had
gotten pregnant.

No, that hadn't been a fun shopping trip. Chloe had
sobbed through the rest of it. Sugar had done all she
could to console her, assuring her that Reid loved her,
that it would all work out for the then seventeen-year-

old Chloe and the eighteen-year-old Reid who had just graduated from high school.

Sugar had been right about Reid. When Chloe had told him the news he'd been shocked, unsettled, shaken up. But he hadn't wavered in his devotion to her.

The baby was only accelerating their plans, he'd said. They were in love, they'd already talked about getting married after college, about having kids and raising them in Northbridge. So what if things would have to be moved up a few years? They'd work everything out.

Reid had even come up with a plan for the best way to tell her difficult parents. They would tell his mother first. His mother, Reid had said, would not be happy with an unplanned, unexpected, teenage pregnancy, but she would stand behind them. And they could enlist the help and support of Reverend Perry, who Chloe's parents respected. With Reid's mother and Reverend Perry behind them, they would tell her parents.

Which was what they went to do on that last night. That awful night.

But in spite of the presence of the reverend and Reid's mother, Chloe's parents hadn't responded well. Her father had been angry and shocked and upset. But her mother had exploded.

Lorene Carmichael wouldn't listen to what anyone had to say. Marriage was out of the question. Chloe had ruined their lives. They would absolutely not allow her to do any more damage than she already had by adding a ridiculous teenage marriage that was doomed to fail to the disastrous situation. Chloe would immediately be sent to her grandparents in Tucson where this would be dealt with outside of the Northbridge gossip mill.

There had been no reasoning with Lorene Carmichael and when the reverend and Mrs. Walker had attempted to, Chloe's mother had ordered them—and Reid—out of her house in a rage that had brought neighbors to their front porches.

"Come with me!" Reid had ordered Chloe when she'd followed him, his mother and the reverend outside, crying and apologizing for the horrible things her mother had said. *"Don't go back in there!"* he'd insisted, holding her tight. *"You can come home with me right now. We can still find a way to be together. To get married. To make this work...."*

Her mother had stormed out of the house then. She'd grabbed Chloe's arm and yanked her from Reid, pulled her back toward the house. And even though Chloe had honestly not known what to do, the fact that Reid's own mother had stepped up, had placed a hand on his arm to stop him from physically taking her out of Lorene's grip, had made Chloe's decision, had reminded her that no matter what Reid said, he was still in the dominion of his family, and she was still in the dominion of hers. And Chloe had gone back into the house.

"You don't look too good."

Reid had been across the room talking to his brother Ad and Chloe hadn't even been aware of his coming back to rejoin her at the group of tables that had been pushed together. But his voice drew her out of her thoughts before she'd revisited more than that last night in Northbridge in her mind.

"Are you sick?" he asked after his initial observation.

"No, I'm fine," Chloe answered him, realizing that she still didn't have any answers to the questions Sugar had left her with. "But I think…"

Did she want to say this? she asked herself.

No, she didn't.

But suddenly it seemed as if she had to. As if there was no other way to calm the confusion Sugar had raised in her.

"…I think maybe we have to talk. Sugar said some things about you and what happened fourteen years ago that I didn't understand. Maybe you can clear them up."

"You want to talk about that here? Now?" Reid asked, clearly even more reluctant than she was, a deep frown pulling his brows close.

Chloe shook her head. "We can't talk with anyone else around."

Reid's eyes held hers for a long moment. She could see that merely mentioning their past was enough to raise some of his darker feelings to the surface again.

But that might be what needed to happen, Chloe told herself. That might be what they needed—to finally bring it all to light.

"Please," she whispered.

Reid took a deep breath and sighed it out. But then he stood. "I hate to be the first one to break up the party," he announced, giving no hint of the exchange he and Chloe had just had. "But I have an early day tomorrow."

Groans and complaints and goading answered him

but Reid tossed it all back and pulled Chloe's chair out for her to stand, too.

"Yeah, yeah, I don't hear any volunteers stepping forward to come by and chip tile off the kitchen wall so nobody gets to give me a hard time," he cajoled as Chloe got to her feet.

"Oh, don't go yet," Sugar said from Chloe's other side.

"I need to, I'm beat," Chloe lied. "But I'll see you again before I leave town."

"Promise," Sugar demanded.

"I promise."

With Chloe and Reid a united front, no more attempts were made to keep them from leaving and instead good-nights were said to pave their way out of Adz.

"I'm parked over there," Reid informed her when they were outside, pointing in the direction they needed to go.

But that was all he said as they walked to his SUV, as he opened the passenger door for her and got in behind the wheel.

That was all either of them said on that short drive that felt miles and miles long.

The moment Reid parked in his driveway, Chloe got out of the car. If they were actually going to talk about what happened fourteen years ago, she wanted to get to it. To get it over with.

"Your place or mine?" Reid asked when he, too, was out of the SUV, an edge to his voice that reminded her of Sunday night.

"Let's go to mine." Because there wouldn't be any chance of his brother coming home and interrupting them.

Reid swept a hand in that direction and Chloe led them across the street, letting them both in her front door.

She took off her coat and so did he, and while Chloe tried to figure out where to start she couldn't help drinking in the tantalizing sight of his snug jeans and the plain navy blue crewneck sweater that managed to cup his shoulders, his beautiful biceps and his well-honed pectorals.

But she wasn't there to be tantalized and as he draped his coat over the carpet roll that still lined the living room wall and then sat on the floor with his back against it, both legs bent at the knee and his forearms braced on top of them, she decided to plunge in.

But not before sitting on the floor in the center of the room because to remain standing there made her feel like a detention teacher facing a rebellious student who didn't want the lecture he was expecting.

"This isn't easy, is it?" she said.

Reid didn't respond to that. Instead he said, "What did Sugar say that you didn't understand?"

"It wasn't *only* what Sugar said. There have been some things with you, too."

"Like what?"

"Well, like that comment you made last night when I said no one's life had been destroyed."

"What didn't you understand about that?"

"Whose life was destroyed?" Chloe asked.

"Come on, Chloe," he said as if he didn't have patience for her playing dumb.

"*Come on?* Really, I don't understand."

"The abortion."

Chloe stopped cold, stunned. "What abortion?"

"The one you had. The one your mother swore she would make you have that night. The one she told me—" He shook his head in what looked like renewed anger and disgust. "The abortion she told me—with such smug satisfaction—that you'd already had by noon the next day."

For a moment Chloe was speechless. She hadn't been playing dumb before but she was dumbstruck now.

When she finally did find her voice, it was quiet. "I didn't have an abortion, Reid. I lost the baby."

He watched her. Studied her. "How?" he challenged.

Chloe wasn't quite sure what to say to that except to outline for him what he *hadn't* been a part of or a witness to that had led up to her losing their baby.

So that's what she did.

"What went on when you and your mom and the reverend were here that last night was nothing compared to what went on after you'd all left. My parents were… They couldn't believe their shining hope for the future had sunk so low—that was one of the things they said. My mother called me horrible names. She broke things. My father wouldn't even look at me, as if I was something so dirty, so foul, he didn't want to know I existed. The fight I had with them was a free-for-all screaming match that went on until after midnight when I said I was going to leave and go to your house."

Chloe couldn't help flinching at that particular memory, recalling how the comment had escalated things.

"Even saying that was like throwing gasoline on a fire. My mother said there was no way I was going anywhere near you ever again. That if I did, she'd have you charged with statutory rape because you were eighteen and I wasn't—"

"The age of consent in Montana is sixteen."

"I didn't know that then. I was convinced my parents could have you sent to jail. Then they said we had to leave Northbridge, that none of us would ever be able to hold our heads up in this town again, that I'd be labeled the town slut, a cheap piece of trash who—"

Chloe hadn't wanted to get into the sordid details and she'd slipped in that direction so she paused and went on without elaborating any more.

"Well, there was a lot of that kind of thing. My parents decided they couldn't even wait until morning, that my father should take me to Billings and put me on a plane for Tucson before I could get anywhere near you again. The next thing I knew, I was in the car with an overnight bag my mother had put in my lap, and I was leaving Northbridge. And you. And there was nothing I could do about it."

Chloe paused and took a few deep breaths to fight back the stress of just retelling this.

Then she continued. "The cramping started about halfway to Billings. I told my father something was wrong but he said I was lying, that if I thought that would get me back to Northbridge I had another thought coming. That nothing was ever getting me back there. By the time we reached Billings I'd started to bleed and he finally took me seriously. I'd lost the baby before we got to the emergency room."

"I can check this out, you know," Reid said, clearly still doubting her.

"Go ahead. I give you permission." She also told him which of Billings' two hospitals her father had taken her to.

For a moment Reid went on staring at her through narrowed eyes, as if he could read the truth in her face. Then he said, "You miscarried," as if she had just told him.

"Yes. My mother said she told you. She said you came to the house first thing the next morning and she told you and you were relieved—"

The laugh Reid let out was devoid of humor. Instead it was full of disbelief, of disgust. "That—"

It was obvious he'd been about to call her mother something not too nice and stopped himself.

After a moment of shaking his head and looking as if he didn't know quite how to react, he said, "Your mother told me that not only had you been willing to have the abortion as soon as possible, but that *you* were relieved that it was all over."

"And you believed her?"

"I was such a wreck and she was so convincing… Yeah, I believed her."

"No, I didn't have an abortion," Chloe felt the need to reiterate. "I miscarried. And I'm sorry, Reid. I'm sorry my mother said—*lied* like that to you. I'm sorry that that's what you were left thinking all this time. And you didn't say anything about it when you came to Tucson two weeks later?"

"Ah, the trip to Tucson," he said with a humorless laugh. "My poor mom," he said, shaking his head at the thought of his own mother. "She didn't want me to do that, that's for sure. She was worried about what your parents would do if I showed up there. But I was full of myself, big on being a man, crazy thinking that you'd been taken away from me, so I packed up and went anyway."

"Your mother was right to be worried."

"Apparently, since your mother called the cops the minute I showed up. She wanted me charged with trespassing and attempted kidnapping of a minor with intent to take you across state lines."

"I know. I heard from my bedroom window upstairs."

"But you didn't come down." There was accusation in that.

"My mother had locked my door before I even knew what was going on. She must have seen you drive up. I couldn't get out. I could just hear what she was saying to the police on the porch below my window. And then I saw them take you off."

"Luckily I had a couple of nice cops. They didn't actually arrest me. They took me in, told me they'd let me go if I left Tucson right then. But if they got another call from your parents about me, they really would arrest me."

"And you still showed up at my school the next day?"

"Yeah," he said. "I slept in my car that night, parked

up the street before dawn the next morning and followed your father and you when he took you. I honestly thought you'd come with me."

But she hadn't. She couldn't. For his sake and for hers. The school security had been on the way. She'd been afraid for him. Afraid of what her parents would do if they found out they hadn't gotten rid of him the day before. Afraid to do what he wanted…

So she'd done what she'd felt she had to do. In the brief moments before school security or the police could get there, she'd told him she didn't love him anymore. That what they'd had was finished. That he needed to go back to Northbridge and they both needed to go on with their lives.

And now that she recalled that, she knew there hadn't been time for him to say anything about the baby.

"That was the first time it hit me," Reid continued in a quiet tone that echoed with a pain that sounded surprisingly strong even now. "The first time it hit me that your mother had been right about everything she'd said that morning in Northbridge. That you'd had an abortion and been happy to do it, to get rid of any connection with me. That you'd been more than willing to get away, to end things with me."

"Oh, that isn't true!"

He pinned her with his eyes. "So you weren't relieved that there wouldn't be a baby?"

Chloe didn't—couldn't—answer that immediately.

There was such powerful accusation in his question that she was tempted to lie. To tell him what she could see he wanted to hear.

But she thought that this was the time for honesty. For complete honesty.

So she steeled herself and confessed. "I was upset and sad, but there was some relief, too. I didn't want to have an abortion and that was a big part of what the fight the night before had been about—I'd refused. But when I lost the baby…I don't know…it seemed like…" She shrugged slightly and begged him with her tone to understand, to put himself in her shoes. "I was seventeen, Reid. I still had another year of high school. My parents were… They could be awful sometimes. You can't tell me you didn't feel a little relief—"

"I felt like punching the smug expression off your mother's face when she told me how she'd made sure a little Walker bastard would never be born. No, I didn't feel relieved. I loved you, Chloe. I *loved* you. Sure, I knew having a baby right then was complicated. But it was *our* baby. Sure, I felt like we were taking on a lot before we were ready for it, but that was okay. It was better than losing you, than not even being an afterthought when it came to whether my own flesh and blood had a chance at life. It was better than ending up with what I ended up with—nothing, not you, not our baby, nothing. Just you telling me I was out there alone—that you didn't love me, that it was over…I nearly went crazy with the frustration, the helplessness, the feeling of *impotence*…"

If he'd hated that feeling as much as he obviously hated saying the word, Chloe thought that it must have eaten him up alive.

He raised his fingertips to his temples, closed his eyes and shook his head again. "I was out-of-my-mind mad." Then he lowered his hands, opened his eyes and let out another no-humor laugh. "And yet I was still hanging on for a while. Hoping you'd just said what you'd said to get me to leave Tucson before things got any worse."

"Which was exactly why I did say what I did."

"But you didn't write. You didn't—"

"I didn't dare write to you. I know you wrote to me. My mother showed me the unopened letters and set them on fire while I watched. But I spent that last year of high school basically under house arrest. My parents didn't let me out of their sight except to go to classes at that private school that was more like a prison—you saw that yourself. I didn't dare make a move that even hinted that I might try to reconnect with you, especially not under the constant threat that my parents would have you thrown in jail. Whether or not it really was a possibility, I *believed* that it was and I was terrified of it."

For a moment neither of them said anything as all the missteps, all the misunderstandings, all the misinformation and misleads hung there between them.

Until Chloe said, "I'm just so, so sorry."

Reid put her on the spot again with that piercing gaze and a look that seemed like a challenge. "What if you *hadn't* thought they could put me in jail? Would you have written? Or tried to get back? Because I keep thinking that a year later you turned eighteen. You were of age. You went to college. You had to have had some freedom, some chance to get hold of me then. But you still didn't."

Chloe hadn't factored in that they would move on from talking about all that *had* happened to what *hadn't.* Or that there would be residual pain and resentment in Reid when they did.

But there it was, in his voice, in those green eyes that once again accused and held her accountable.

"I thought about it," Chloe said.

"Thinking about it isn't doing it."

"I know."

"So why didn't you?"

It took her a moment to answer him and when she did she couldn't look at him; she had to glance away.

"I still wasn't sure if there was anything my parents could do to you legally, so that was a factor. But by then… Well, a year had passed. So much had happened and changed. I'd moved on and I thought you must have, too—especially after what I'd said to you in Tucson to make you leave. I assumed you'd gone through with your plans to go to Northbridge College. I was enrolled in the university in Tucson…"

That was all true but it was still dancing around what he wanted to know.

Chloe sighed and gave it. "I was afraid. I didn't want to come back, to test my mother's theory that I'd be in for a huge helping of scorn. What we'd had had ended badly. It didn't seem likely or realistic to think we had any kind of future, that anything we'd talked about as starry-eyed kids would actually have a chance of happening. And there was that big, awful ugliness of the pregnancy and the miscarriage and the scene that last night here and everything that had happened in Tucson—it just seemed better to leave it all alone. I honestly thought that was probably what you thought, too."

Reid didn't say anything and that silence made Chloe feel defensive and in need of reasoning with him.

"We were *kids,* Reid. Kids when we got together. Kids when we got into trouble. We weren't much more than that a year later. There was still college we both wanted to get through and a whole lot more growing up to do. I just kept thinking, *What if I did go back?* Picturing it, you know?"

He didn't give any indication of understanding but Chloe went on anyway.

"I kept picturing my coming back here and I didn't see how it could be good. My parents swore that if I ever had anything to do with you again they'd disown me. That they would be through with me forever. And you know how they were—they would have done it. And I kept thinking what if I risked that and came here to find that I really was looked at as the returning town slut and you didn't want me anymore and then I wouldn't be able to go back with my parents either and—" She blew out a big breath. "I just thought it was best to leave things as they were."

Reid nodded but she could see none of what she'd said had convinced him she had been right in staying away, in not contacting him at all.

"I'm sorry," she said again. "I'm sorry if I was wrong. But on the other hand, if any of this had been done differently, if we had gotten married that summer or gotten back together the next year and gone from there, would we still be together now? Would you be a doctor today? Or would we both have ended up without our educations and as part of the divorce statistics for teenage marriages?"

"I guess we'll never know, will we?"

"I think things happen the way they're meant to."

He appeared to consider that for a moment before he shrugged one shoulder and one eyebrow at the same time. Then he said, "Maybe you're right. After all, it looks like you were more the levelheaded one and I was the hopeless romantic."

A joke. A small, wry joke, but a joke.

That seemed like a positive sign.

"I don't know how levelheaded I was," Chloe said, trying out a tiny smile on him.

"I don't think you were quite the romantic I was," he said, answering her smile with one of his own.

"And now it's all history."

"That's true," he agreed.

"Can we still let bygones be bygones?"

Once more he took a moment before answering. Then, on the exhale of a sigh, he said, "I think we can probably do better than that. It's good to know what really went down all those years ago. Good but draining," he added, looking and sounding as exhausted as Chloe felt.

And for some reason she had the sense that not everything had been resolved between them despite the fact that she thought they'd gone over all there was to rehash. Not that Reid was doing or saying anything to make her feel that way, or that she had any idea what could have been left *un*resolved at that point. It was just a feeling she had.

But when Reid got to his feet, put on his coat and changed the subject, she decided she must be imagining things, that it must just have been unsettling to have delved into the past.

"My mom is fixing a big family dinner tomorrow night. I thought you might like to come," he said on his way to the door.

"A big family dinner on a Thursday night? What's the occasion? Someone's birthday?" she asked, going with him.

"There are reasons I can't divulge," he said, making it sound overly mysterious.

"Reasons that have to do with me?" Chloe probed, her mother's insistences that she would be treated badly in this town lingering in the back of her mind even now.

"Nope. Other reasons…"

Reid even wiggled his eyebrows up and down that time, making Chloe laugh.

"Not only do I have the lure of your mom's cooking but now you have me too curious to say no," she said.

"Then you'll come."

"I guess I will."

"Good."

"So are you really prying tile off the kitchen wall tomorrow?" she asked.

"I am. But since it's noisier than painting I won't start too early. How about the attic? How are you coming with that?"

"I finished going through everything and sorting it. Tomorrow I'll get it all ready to go out. On Friday I have someone from the church coming for the charity stuff, and I'm paying the trash haulers to cart the throwaways out of the attic. They'll recycle what can be recycled and dispose of the rest for me. What I'm keeping I'll pack up and mail to myself."

Reid nodded but Chloe had the impression he wasn't paying too much attention to what she was saying. Not that his interest wasn't on her, because it was. He hadn't taken his eyes off her. And again she wondered if everything from their past actually was resolved.

"So...are we okay?" she asked.

"I'm okay. Are you okay?" he answered as if he didn't know what she was talking about, again making her wonder if she were just imagining that he was still harboring something.

"I'm okay," she said. "I'm glad we got everything out in the open."

"Yeah, me, too," he agreed.

Then, he reached out and took both of her upper arms in his big hands, rubbing up and down.

"I wish things had been different," he admitted. "But otherwise, I'm glad we got everything out in the open now, too. I'm glad to know—even after all this time—that you didn't end the pregnancy without so much as a word to me, as if I hadn't had any part in it. I think it'll just take me a little time to sort through it all and let go of what I believed happened for so long."

"*Can* you let go of it?" Chloe asked quietly.

"Now that I know the truth? I can't see why not."

He wasn't letting go of her, though.

His hands were still on her arms, in one place now, his thumbs doing a gentle massage that was working wonders in the way of relaxing her, in lulling her out of the tension that had gone with talking about the past.

It also didn't hurt anything that she was looking up into his starkly handsome face, into eyes that had softened to hold a hint of warmth again.

A warmth and a softness that hadn't even been in them the night before when she'd thought he might kiss her.

But it was there now. And so were thoughts of his kissing her. Only unlike the last two nights, tonight Reid kissing her seemed more than possible. It seemed imminent.

Then he did it. He kissed her.

But only on the forehead, where he pressed his lips for several moments before he straightened up and peered down into her eyes again.

"I'm sorry you had to go through what you did, too," he said, quietly, sincerely. "I'm sorry that your folks weren't more understanding or compassionate. That your mother made you feel like some kind of scarlet woman who shouldn't show her face here again. I'm sorry that you had to deal with a miscarriage without any support. At seventeen. I'm sorry that the one time we were together, which was so nice, had such lousy consequences and that I couldn't be with you through all of them."

He would never guess how much it meant to her to have him say that. To have him recognize that it *had* been awful for her fourteen years ago. To have him finally put aside his own old hurts and recognize hers.

"Let's both let go of it," he suggested. "Let's both forgive ourselves and each other and honestly put it behind us."

Chloe breathed a sigh of relief. "I'd like that. You can't know how much I'd like that."

"It's done then. Gone. *Poof!* Up in smoke," he said, injecting a bit of levity that helped, too.

"Good riddance," Chloe contributed with flair.

"Good riddance," he agreed.

Chloe actually did feel a weight lift off her shoulders. A huge, heavy weight that she'd been carrying around for far too long. A huge, heavy weight that finally convinced her that everything *was* resolved between them.

Still Reid had a hold of her arms. Still he was looking down at her.

Then he leaned forward and pulled her toward him at the same time, only not to merely kiss her forehead this time.

Instead his mouth met hers in a kiss that at first was much like the one that had preceded it—simple and chaste.

But where it began was not where it went.

The kiss seemed to deepen on its own. Reid's lips parted and so did Chloe's and suddenly it wasn't a friendly, comforting, reconnecting kind of kiss. Suddenly it was a real kiss that banished any doubt that there was nothing of the old flames left between them.

Reid did release his hold on her then. But only to

wrap his arms around her. And somehow Chloe's hands found their way to his broad, hard back, too, as mouths opened a bit wider and bodies met front-to-front—if only barely.

And all of the wondering Chloe had done about what Reid's kisses might be like now, all the wondering she'd done about whether or not they would be different, came to an end as she learned—in glorious detail—that they both were and weren't. There was old and new at once. Some things about that kiss were what she remembered, what she'd relived a trillion times in her mind over the years; and other things were so much more experienced, so much more confident, so much more adept and polished and better.

So, so much better…

So much better that Chloe didn't want to ever stop kissing him. She didn't want him to ever stop kissing her.

But that was hardly realistic and even though she still hadn't actually had her fill, the kiss did end. Slowly and with a couple of lingering returns before Reid straightened up again, replaced his hands on her arms and, as if he were using them as leverage, pushed himself a step away from her.

Chloe wasn't sure what was going to happen then. Was he going to express regrets or say they shouldn't have done that and shouldn't ever do it again?

But Reid merely smiled a smile that crinkled the corners of his eyes and said, "See you tomorrow."

Chloe nodded, not wanting to talk, wanting to keep the feel of his mouth on hers as long as she could.

Then Reid opened the door and stepped outside, closing it behind himself.

Chloe just went on standing there, lost yet in that kiss that had been a combination of familiarity and the new and improved. Lost and happy that it hadn't disappointed—and oh, boy, had it not disappointed!

And even moments later, when she finally locked the door and headed for bed, she was still thinking about that kiss.

That kiss that had left her feeling more thoroughly, more sublimely, kissed than she'd felt in fourteen years.

That kiss that made her hope that the bad parts of their past genuinely had been put to rest.

Chapter Eight

Prying ceramic tile off a wall, Reid discovered, was time-consuming work that occupied the hands more than the mind. Sure, he had a radio he kept on and tuned to the local station, but on Thursday not even that provided a distraction from rehashing all he and Chloe had talked about the evening before.

Although he would never want Chloe to know he'd done it, very early that morning he'd made a call to a friend from medical school who was on staff at the hospital in Billings where Chloe had said she'd gone when she'd miscarried. His friend had looked up the old records and confirmed that it was true—she had, indeed, been brought into the emergency room in the final stages of an early-term miscarriage.

Reid felt guilty for checking up on her, but after

fourteen years of believing something, he'd needed that confirmation to seal the deal and honestly do that letting go they'd talked about. He'd needed that confirmation to readjust his thinking.

And that was what he was doing as he tore off tile.

In the hours since Chloe had told him her side of what had happened, he'd realized that in the last fourteen years he'd primarily thought of himself, of how he'd felt, of what he'd gone through, of how he'd been wronged.

How he'd been dumped.

Now he saw that Chloe had gone through a hell of her own. And that she'd had reasons for why she'd opted to do what her parents approved of.

But he still couldn't help wishing that even though it was something she'd almost never done before the pregnancy, she would have rebelled once that had happened. That she would have left her own house that night and come to his no matter what it had taken. That she would have come to *him*. That she would have gone against her parents, because their baby and being together would have been more important to her.

Because she'd been more important to him. Important enough for him to face her parents that night. To chase her to Tucson. To even ignore the warning of the cops there that they'd throw the book at him if they found him anywhere near Chloe or the Carmichaels again.

And what that told him, he decided as he worked, was what he'd thought all along. That even though it might have seemed as if Chloe had felt about him the way he'd felt about her, she hadn't.

He supposed it was good to have that confirmed, too. Because while his youthful feelings for her had long ago dissolved, he couldn't deny that there was some attraction to her blossoming all over again now. And knowing that she hadn't felt about him the way he'd felt about her seemed like a tool for him to use to keep that attraction in check. Which was exactly what he intended to do.

So it was nice to know that Chloe hadn't lied to him, or done something as big as an abortion without regard to him. Knowing that went a long way in helping him put that portion of their past behind him. But he didn't want to let go of *all* of their past. Some of it he wanted to keep in mind as a safety net.

Because when it came to Chloe, he needed one.

He wished that weren't the case, but it was. And as much as he would have liked to deny it, he couldn't very well do that after the last three nights. After the *end* of the last three nights. Particularly after the end of *last* night.

There was something about saying good-night to her that was like turning back a clock. And no matter how careful he'd been up to that point to keep some distance—not to notice how incredible she looked or smelled, to ignore the fact that just the sound of her voice touched a place inside him that was softer than he wanted to admit—no matter how hard he tried to fight the little chill that ran along the surface of his skin every time she smiled, the ends of the evenings put a chink in the armor he was trying to keep on.

Monday and Tuesday night had been bad enough. Monday he'd only been thinking about kissing her. Remembering how incredible it had been to kiss her fourteen years ago—so incredible that if he'd been able to keep his lips locked on to hers twenty-four hours a day he would have.

But those thoughts and memories notwithstanding, he hadn't acted on them and that was what counted.

Tuesday night he'd come closer. He'd actually caught himself leaning in a little. But he'd overcome the urge and pulled back before it had gone too far.

And then there was Wednesday night.

Last night.

Damn if he hadn't done it.

One minute he'd been trying to let her know he finally recognized that what had happened fourteen years ago hadn't been a breeze for her either, and that he was sorry for what she'd been through. One minute he'd been looking for a little closure for them both.

And the next minute he'd gone nuts and given in to what he'd fought the two nights before. He'd kissed her. A big-time, no-kidding-around, full-on kiss that had sure as hell had nothing to do with closure.

Plus, to make matters worse, it had been a great kiss. Every bit as good as the best kisses they'd ever shared and better. A lot better.

That was when he'd known that regardless of how much he wanted to deny that he was attracted to her— and not just to the memory of her or because of something they'd had together a long time ago—he couldn't. Because it was there and real and it had the capacity to make him do things that he knew he shouldn't do.

So, yeah, he definitely needed a safety net.

And that safety net was the realization that their feelings for each other hadn't matched up fourteen years ago. If they hadn't matched up fourteen years ago they likely wouldn't ever match up, and he had the potential for getting in deeper than she would.

And he wasn't going to let that happen. No way. No how. Not now. Not ever again.

It had been too painful.

It had put him in a place he never wanted to be again as long as he lived.

And it had led him to do other things he wasn't proud of.

No doubt about it, there was one part of the past he wasn't letting go of.

The part that would keep him from falling for Chloe.

That part he was going to hang on to for dear life.

In spite of how great Wednesday night's kiss was, in the cold light of day Thursday Chloe knew it had been a mistake. She and Reid were inching toward a new relationship and kissing was just too big a leap. Whether it was a leap forward or a leap backward, she didn't know, but either way, it wasn't something that should have happened.

And knowing that left her not quite sure what to do. Which was why she was once again avoiding him and hiding out in the attic, eating a dry sandwich for lunch—a dry sandwich she'd run to the kitchen to make in a hurry only when she'd heard Reid leave the house. She wanted a clear head when she saw him again and so far that wasn't what she had.

So far what she had were a whole bunch of urges that certainly weren't clarifying. The urge to greet him with another kiss, for instance. The urge to touch him. To have him touch her. To hold hands with him. To do much, much more than hold hands with him...

Definitely not clearheaded thinking. And that was dangerous.

It was just that that kiss had tapped into a sort of Pandora's box that Chloe had been sitting on since she'd left Northbridge. The Pandora's box where she'd stuffed her feelings for Reid.

She'd had to do something with them or she would never have been able to get through those early days and months after her parents had ushered her out of Northbridge.

Being pregnant at seventeen had been terrifying in spite of the fact that she'd had a boyfriend who had been determined to do right by her. A boyfriend who had seemed to have no obvious qualms about rushing into a teenage marriage. Chloe had still needed the security of her family, even a family that wasn't the most compassionate or understanding.

Yes, she'd been in love with Reid. As madly in love as any seventeen-year-old girl could be. And yes, before the pregnancy, she'd been sure they would be together until the end of time.

But then the pregnancy had happened and she'd been brought up short by how serious things could become. Had she felt some relief when she'd miscarried? Yes. She saw that that hadn't been something Reid had wanted to hear, but it was true. Once she *had* lost the baby she'd admitted to herself that there was no way she'd been prepared or eager to have a child.

Which was probably why, during the first few weeks in Arizona she'd begun to take some of what her parents had said to heart. To sort through it and decide what they were right about. And what they were right about was that she and Reid *were* very young. What her parents were right about was that they both needed to go on with school, to grow up, before marriage and babies entered the picture.

And so she'd taken those intense feelings she'd had for Reid and put them away, sealing the lid on them.

The feelings had never completely gone away, though, and kissing him last night, wanting to kiss him again today, alerted her to the fact that there still were feelings for him.

But as she sat in the attic considering it all, she knew that she couldn't let those feelings run free. Because although she might have hoped that the kiss they'd shared the night before had been a sign that their past had been put to rest, when she'd woken up this morning she'd again had that unsettled feeling. And as she'd worked, she'd realized what it was that was niggling at her.

Yes, their past and all the misunderstandings and even her mother's lies had been brought out into the open and, hopefully, resolved. But there was something else that couldn't be.

There was the fact that Reid had spent fourteen years as a bubbling cauldron of anger and resentment.

There was the fact that not only did she and Reid have a history, they had a history with hard feelings.

And hard feelings were different from the feelings she'd harbored and hidden away in her Pandora's box. Hard feelings were something else entirely. Something that Chloe had learned about more recently on her own.

What she'd learned about hard feelings was that no amount of talking, apologizing or making amends ever really dissolved them. It might temporarily soften them—which was probably what had brought Reid to the point of kissing her. But it never really, completely dissolved them. And the lid on the Pandora's box that contained hard feelings? Nothing could keep that down forever.

A clear head—that was what she'd set out for today and that was what she got. The kind of clearheadedness she'd had a few days earlier—before kissing had entered the picture—when she'd told herself that she and Reid could be only friendly acquaintances. Because the more she thought about the resentment and anger she'd seen in him on Sunday night, the anger that had been so close to the surface even the night before that he'd had trouble believing she'd had a miscarriage rather than an abortion, the more she knew that she really couldn't let things between them go any further than they already had.

Chloe set down her half-eaten sandwich. Her appetite had disappeared.

Because coming to the conclusion once again that there couldn't be anything between her and Reid sent an overwhelming sadness through her.

She knew that was uncalled for. After all, she hadn't come to Northbridge with any intention of even seeing Reid, let alone rekindling anything.

But sadness was there anyway. And regret. Regret that now that she *had* seen him again, now that she knew what kind of man he'd become, how incredible he was and how strongly she was still attracted to him, they *could* only be friendly acquaintances. Or maybe, at best, just friends.

Chloe sighed resignedly, making herself accept that friendship at best was the wisest route. The only route around fourteen years of hard feelings.

And now that she knew she had to take that route, she also thought that she should beg off of tonight's dinner with Reid and his family.

She should stay right where she was, concentrate on the work in the attic in order to finish it ahead of schedule so she could get out of this whole situation. Out of this house, out of close proximity to Reid and out of Northbridge with as little further contact with him as she could manage.

But the thought of that made her even sadder. Morose, almost, to think that she couldn't so much as have a simple meal with Reid and the rest of the Walkers.

She'd enjoyed getting out a little in Northbridge and seeing some of the people who had been important to her young life. And she really wanted to see his mom again...

So what if she hung on tight to her resolve that she and Reid couldn't be anything but friends and looked at tonight as nothing more than that—dinner with friends? Could she let herself go then?

She shouldn't.

But she wanted to so much...

So much that she couldn't help giving herself a little leeway.

It *was* dinner with Reid and a whole bunch of other people, not dinner alone with him. Wasn't a group dinner like group dating—less risky?

And if she absolutely promised herself that she wouldn't let there be anything else to the evening? Couldn't she do it?

Bargaining with herself—she was actually bargaining with herself.

She closed her eyes and said forcefully, "I swear I'll behave," as if someone else were there to hear it.

And then she granted herself permission.

To go to Reid's family dinner as friends—and *only* friends—with Reid.

Because it was friends or nothing, she thought, giving herself that ultimatum.

Friends or nothing...

She couldn't forget that.

And if she even started to, she swore she'd remind herself of how hard Reid's feelings had been.

And of just how awful things between them could end up if she didn't take their impact seriously enough.

When Reid came to get Chloe at seven, she was waiting, watching for him through the living room window.

She was freshly showered and shampooed, dressed in a pair of jeans and a form-fitting black sweater with a ballet neckline. Her face was carefully made-up with just the right hints of blush and mascara, and she'd left her hair to fall in licorice-colored waves around her shoulders—the way she would have dressed to have dinner with any friend.

"Hey, stranger, where've you been all day?" Reid called to her when she opened the door as he started up the drive.

"I was busy in the attic," she answered, grateful that there were no clues in her voice to give away the fact that one glance at him had put the memory of that kiss back in her head as if it had just happened.

As Reid continued his approach, Chloe took in what he was wearing. She was happy to see that he was in jeans and a snug heather-gray mock-neck T-shirt that showed off his broad shoulders and muscular chest to good effect. Well, she wasn't happy that that T-shirt showed off the impressive proportions of his torso to such good effect that it made her hands itch to be pressed to his honed pectorals. She was just happy to find that her own clothes weren't too casual for the occasion.

"I'm glad I wasn't supposed to dress up for this," she said as she let him into the house. "I didn't pack for anything fancy."

"It's just dinner at Mom's," he assured.

"Does she know I'm coming?" Chloe asked, concerned suddenly with how the would-have-been-grandmother of the baby she'd lost might feel about her.

"It was her idea to invite you," Reid said.

"So, there's no ill will?"

"All water under the bridge. She's looking forward to seeing you."

"I'm looking forward to seeing her, too," Chloe said honestly because she'd always been genuinely fond of his mother and *had* been looking forward to seeing Lotty Walker until it had occurred to her that the older woman might have some hard feelings of her own.

"I must have gone out of here without my coat this afternoon. I couldn't find it at home," Reid said then, glancing around until he located it draped over the roll of carpeting.

Chloe had laid her own jacket at the opposite end of the roll and when he saw it, he bypassed his to pick up hers, holding it for her to slip into.

"You first," he suggested.

"Thanks," Chloe said, turning around to accommodate the help.

The clean scent of his cologne drifted to her when he stepped close enough to finesse the jacket over her shoulders and that didn't help her efforts to keep this on a strictly friendly basis because it spurred an instant fantasy of him wrapping his arms around her from there. Of him kissing her neck. Of her leaning back and feeling that big body of his right up against hers…

Just friends. Just friends, she chanted to herself, thinking that that was the problem with kissing—it stirred things up that shouldn't be stirred up and made control harder to accomplish.

But Chloe was determined. Friends or nothing, she reminded herself, stiffening her spine and pretending nothing had been stirred up at all as she stepped away from Reid.

She faced him again as he retrieved his jean jacket

and put it on, apparently unaware of what had been going through her mind, and equally unaware of how the sight of his chest thrust forward when he shrugged into his coat affected her, too.

"I assumed we'd just walk up to your mom's?" she said, her voice tinged with an aloofness that went along with her ramrod posture and her attempts to find a way *not* to be so affected by him tonight.

Reid smiled as if she'd said something amusing. "You *assumed* that, did you?" he said, making fun of the stilted way she'd asked the question.

Chloe raised her chin at him and toughed out his teasing. "Yes, I assumed."

"I *assumed* we would, too," he said. Then he pivoted on his heels, swept a long arm in the direction of her door, and said a formal, "After you."

Chloe couldn't help laughing at him and it helped take some of the starch out of her.

The bracing autumn air helped, too, and while she was waiting for Reid to close the front door behind them she took a deep breath, feeling a little lighter when she released it, as if she were releasing the stress that had been her companion all day as well.

They headed across the yard toward the street, falling into step beside each other when they reached the sidewalk.

"So who will be here tonight? Only your family?" Chloe asked, trying not to think of the innumerable strolls she'd taken with him long ago, holding hands or with Reid's arm around her and her tucked neatly beneath it….

"Only the family but the family is extending, as I'm sure you noticed at Adz after the game last night, even if you were preoccupied and kept under Sugar's wing," Reid answered.

"It still seems strange that everyone is grown up now. I mean, I know we are, so of course everyone else is, too. But I always picture everyone here the way they were when I saw them the last time. So in my head your brothers and sister are so much younger. But here they are—I can't believe Ad is married—"

"To Kit, who's a famous baker of wedding cakes," Reid supplied as if he were reminding her in case she'd forgotten since the night before.

"Ben is an upstanding citizen after all his wayward antics as a kid—"

"And married to Clair Cabot—I don't know if you remember her, she was Ben's age—so a little younger than you—and her dad owned the school for boys."

"I do remember her. We talked last night. I had a gym class with her. She told me about getting together with Ben at their reunion and then reconnecting when he bought the school for troubled kids. And apparently they're having a baby?"

"A reunion souvenir. Unplanned—so see, it happens to the best of us."

But it was nice that that unplanned pregnancy had worked out for his brother because Chloe had seen how happy Ben and Clair were together.

Reid leaned slightly to the side then and said, "This is strictly confidential—Cassie is our surprise guest tonight."

"Your sister is in town?"

"As of this afternoon. She and Joshua Cantrell flew in in a helicopter that landed out in the middle of nowhere so no one would know they were here yet. That's why we're all having dinner tonight. You know who Joshua Cantrell is, don't you?"

"Who doesn't? His name gets splashed around as much as Donald Trump's. Joshua Cantrell is the Titan of Tennis Shoes. Didn't I see a picture on the front of some awful tabloid a few weeks ago of your sister sprawled across the top of a brick wall around his property?"

"You and everybody else," Reid said wryly. "Cassie had broken up with Joshua and then had second thoughts. She was trying to get to him without press coverage but didn't quite make it."

"How did she ever meet him?"

"Mmm, I can't tell. But they're here now and they're trying to keep it quiet as long as they can."

"I promise not to sell the information," Chloe assured him as they went up the steps to the front porch where they'd spent many evenings sitting on the swing that hung from chains. Where they'd spent many evenings making out...

No, no kissing, Chloe silently insisted, once again forcing the memory of the previous evening's end out of her head.

Reid opened his mother's front door and the sounds of voices and kitchen noise announced that the Walker family really had been extended enough for there to be a crowd inside.

But at that moment it was a welcome prospect to Chloe.

Because it looked as though she needed all the distractions she could get not to think about Reid and things that were a whole lot steamier than friendship.

Chapter Nine

"That's all, folks," Ben announced at the end of the long string of home movies that had been the after-dinner entertainment.

Reid and Luke pretended to be thankful that the movies were finally over while Joshua Cantrell whistled and applauded as if he'd just watched a blockbuster.

Chloe smiled at the whole scene, having had one of the best evenings she could remember since arriving at the Walkers' home for the family dinner she'd wanted to attend too much to deny herself.

"I'd forgotten how many of the movies you were in, Chloe," Cassie said then. "I'm so glad you were here to see them with us."

"It looked like you were one of the family," Ad's wife, Kit, contributed.

"We all thought she was going to be," Ben said.

From beside Chloe on the sofa, Lotty Walker patted Chloe's knee. "I consider her one of the family even if we don't get to see her."

Chloe appreciated that easy out of what could have been awkward.

Joshua Cantrell's eighteen-year-old sister, Alyssa, stretched and yawned then from where she was sitting on the floor. "I don't know about anybody else, but I need to get some sleep before tomorrow's... Before tomorrow."

Everyone else began to relay the same sentiments since it was nearly midnight, getting up from their various movie seats around the room.

The dinner dishes had been done earlier so with the exception of a few glasses and coffee cups that Lotty insisted be left right where they were until morning, there was nothing to be cleaned up. So when Luke came back from retrieving coats from one of the bedrooms upstairs they were passed out and put on.

"Oh, Chloe, let me get your goodies!" Lotty said, half-running for the kitchen as everyone else converged on the front door with Cassie and Joshua Cantrell bringing up the rear because they were staying there.

Lotty hurried back with more containers than she could comfortably carry and Ben—who was nearest to the back of the group—lunged just in time to catch one of them from falling. Then he divided them between Chloe and Reid.

"You really didn't have to do all this." Chloe repeated what she'd said several times since dinner when Lotty had decreed that she'd be sending leftovers with her.

"It's nothing," Lotty insisted. "Freeze what you can't eat right away and you can take it back to Arizona with you. The fudge and peanut brittle will stay a long time even without being frozen."

"Okay. Well, thank you," Chloe said.

No one else needed to bring anything home because they would all be back at Lotty's at some point or an-other in the near future, and recognizing that made Chloe feel slightly like an outsider. But she tried not to dwell on that and concentrated on the fact that she'd had a wonderful evening as she received a big hug from the older woman.

"I hope we'll get to see you again. Tomorrow maybe," Lotty said.

Chloe didn't have a clue what was going on the next day but between Alyssa Cantrell's comment and Lotty's, she was beginning to think that something was.

She didn't know what to say to her hostess's remark, however, so she merely thanked Lotty once again for the meal, the take-homes, and the evening.

Alyssa lingered inside talking to Joshua and Cassie, but outside Ad and his wife and Ben and his wife said good-night and headed for their cars, while Luke, Reid and Chloe started up the street.

Along the way the three of them had a few laughs reminiscing about a water fight that had been in one of the movies, and over clothes and hairstyles that had been caught on film. Then they reached their end of the block. Luke said good-night and crossed to the house he and Reid lived in, and Reid and Chloe went to Chloe's.

"I can't believe how much food your mom sent," Chloe said with a laugh as they balanced containers in order to get the front door unlocked and opened. "I'll be eating for a month on all this," she added once they were inside.

"Mom thought you looked too thin," Reid said, turning on the kitchen light with his elbow and taking things to the counter beside the refrigerator. "I, on the other hand, think you look great."

It was a simple compliment and yet it managed to give Chloe a little charge that she tried to subdue by reminding herself they could only be friends.

It was hardly the first time tonight that she'd had to do that because even being with the rest of Reid's family hadn't kept her from focusing totally on him. It hadn't kept her from noticing how great *he* looked every chance she got to see him at a distance. No amount of distraction had made it possible for her not to hang on his every word. Not to feel a rush every time he'd leaned over and shared a private joke with her or touched her even in some completely innocuous way.

In fact, being at a Walker family event—much as she had often when they were dating as kids—being seated beside him for the meal and during the movies, having him take special care in making sure her needs were attended to and that she was included in every conversation, had made it seem like they *were* more than friends. Like they were a couple again.

Something that no amount of reminders that they weren't seemed to change.

And now here they were, back home together, just the two of them. And no matter what she told herself, being with him like that made her feel that they were more than friends.

"Were you okay with that part-of-the-family talk at the end?" Reid asked, drawing Chloe out of her musings as he opened the fridge and they began to load it by Chloe handing him things and him putting them inside.

"Oh, sure. It was no big deal," she said.

"And how about all the are-you-married questions? I think I heard that at least four times."

"Again, no big deal," Chloe assured, handing him the last of the containers.

She thought Reid would probably say good-night himself then—not that she wanted him to, but it *was* getting late.

Only instead of doing that he shut the refrigerator door and surprised her by pulling a bottle of wine out of the side pocket of his jacket.

"Where'd you get that?" she asked with a laugh.

"From Mom's. There's only about two glasses left but it's good wine and I hated to see it thrown out. So I snagged it."

"I didn't even see it in your pocket."

Reid grinned a mischievous grin. "Neither did anybody else. I can be sly when I want. I thought we could round things off with a nightcap. Unless you're tired…"

"No, a nightcap sounds good."

The agreement was spontaneous. Completely without forethought. On impulse. The impulse to prolong this time with him…

"Grab a couple of paper cups," he suggested, returning to the living room.

With cups in hand, Chloe followed Reid, finding him removing his jacket. She set the cups down and took off hers, too, and they both sat on the floor, angled against the carpet roll, facing each other in the dimness of the room lit only by the light coming from the kitchen.

Reid divided the wine evenly between the two cups and handed her one of them.

He took a drink and then leveled those blue-tinged-green eyes at her. "Okay, so in conjunction with the are-you-married question," he said then. "What have you been doing with yourself on that front in the last fourteen years?"

"Nothing like getting to the point," Chloe countered with a laugh at his blatant interest.

Reid shrugged. "You can't blame me for being curious. I just wasn't sure I wanted to know the gory details until now."

There *was* something different about him tonight, she thought. He was more relaxed. More playful. More the temperament he'd been long ago. It was as if their talk the previous evening had released some of the tension in him. As if it had freed him to be himself.

And Chloe liked it so much. It suddenly seemed like old times—like the best of the old times—and that had such a potent appeal...

"In the attic when we were talking about the broken arrow and the bottle of rain," he said then. "You told me that was the most romantic thing anybody had ever done and I've been wondering what *has* gone on with your love life ever since."

"And now you're ready for the gory details?"

"They'd better be gory, too. I don't want to hear anything about great guys or superstars."

Chloe laughed. "Are you telling me you're jealous?"

"I was the guy you kicked to the curb, remember? Don't tell me you dumped me and went on to greener pastures. I want to hear about guys with crooked teeth and jock itch who couldn't grow a full beard if they had to."

Chloe laughed. "There was a guy here and there who came close to that but those were blind dates I never saw again. And I haven't done a *whole* lot of dating. I was a little gun-shy even when my parents let me anywhere near boys again."

And since most of the men she'd met hadn't lived up to her memories of Reid, she'd kept to herself more than anything. But she wasn't going to tell him that.

"How long would you say you were gun-shy? Until last month?" Reid asked, obviously joking but his tone tinged with a hint of hope, too.

Chloe laughed. "Maybe not quite that long. But there was only one guy who was more than a few-dates kind of relationship. Thad—short for Theodore Martin Russell the third."

"Pedigreed? I'll bet your mother approved."

"He was and she did. Thad was from a family of real estate moguls. They own a chunk of Tucson, and Thad is in the process of building and acquiring an empire of his own."

"Were things serious with Thad?"

"Pretty serious. We did eventually get engaged."

It was strange talking about this with Reid, of all people. But now that they'd begun, there didn't seem like a way out of it. Especially when he persisted.

"Why *eventually?*" he asked, repeating what she'd said.

"We were together about eight years. Off and on. Up until a year ago. His mother and mine did charity work together and they arranged for us to meet."

"An arranged meeting with the man of her choice—that sounds like it was right up your mother's alley. And was it love at first sight for you and the Thad-man?"

Chloe could say that about Reid but not about Thad. "No, I liked him all right—he was attractive and had a good sense of humor and he seemed more down to earth than the rest of his family, so when he asked me out I accepted and it grew from there."

"Off and on," Reid reminded. "How come?"

Chloe shrugged, once more reluctant to let him know he'd played a role—or at least the memory of him had.

"Let's just say lingering gun-shyness. Every time he'd get serious, I'd pull back and we'd take a break."

Chloe had finished her wine and she set the cup on the floor, out of the way.

"So how did you end up engaged?"

"About two years ago we'd taken another break and it had followed the same pattern—we'd keep in touch, have lunch or dinner occasionally and before too long we'd ease into seeing each other steadily again. Only that time Thad said enough was enough, he wanted to get married, he thought if we finally made a firm commitment to each other, we'd move forward instead of the back-and-forth stuff."

"And you said yes."

"Not immediately. I thought about it for a while. But Thad was—sorry, but he was—a good guy, and I really had come to care about him. I decided I just had to get over—"

Get over you...

That's what she'd almost said. She'd caught herself in the nick of time. But at least she had caught herself.

Regrouping in a hurry, she went on. "I just had to get over being gun-shy once and for all. I thought that maybe Thad was right, we should just take the leap and get on with things."

"So you said yes," Reid said very quietly.

"I said yes," Chloe confirmed.

"Then you got cold feet?" he asked, stretching an arm along the top of the carpet roll behind her but not touching her.

"Nooo..." Chloe said. "Then I showed up at his office unexpectedly one afternoon and found him and his new secretary in a clinch."

Reid's eyebrows rose. "That does not sound like a good guy."

"He was a good guy before that. And he swore he wasn't having a full-blown affair. But he confessed that he was attracted to Adele—that was her name—and having second thoughts about me."

"Goodbye, Thad."

Chloe made a face. "Actually, not completely. I went a little crazy."

That surprised him. "You?"

"It was just this weird thing—Thad had always been available and I'd taken that for granted. Through every breakup I'd known that one phone call from me would bring him running back whenever I wanted. But suddenly there was the chance that I might lose him and—"

"You wanted him."

"I did," she said, again thinking how weird it was to be saying this to Reid.

"So what did you do?"

"I decided not to give up without a fight." But Chloe was absolutely not going to reveal any details of how she went about that. Instead she skipped to the end result of her efforts. "And after about three weeks, Thad decided I was who he wanted, too. That he'd just had a brief lapse in judgment, probably brought on by those cold feet you mentioned, and it was goodbye, Adele."

"The wedding was on again."

"It was. Plans were set into motion. Thad and I moved in together—we hadn't lived together before, it was something else I'd dragged my feet about. But I agreed to move into his house and I thought I'd dodged the bullet of losing Thad."

"But you hadn't?"

"I'm not proud of this," she admitted reluctantly. "All the while we were split up over Adele I was only thinking one thing—get back with Thad. I buried everything else I felt. But the longer we were back together, and the closer the wedding got, the more I realized just how much I'd resented what he'd done. How much it had rocked me that he'd gotten involved with someone else when we weren't even on a break, when he was *engaged* to me. That he'd finally gotten what he'd said he wanted—for me to say I'd marry him—and the minute he had, he'd gone behind my back and lied to me to see someone else. That I'd been reduced to trying to win some dumb competition for him—"

"You were hurt, angry and resentful," Reid summed up, obviously connecting what she'd experienced with Thad to what he'd felt for the last fourteen years.

"Yes," Chloe confirmed. "I didn't have any idea until then how crazy rejection could make me, but I guess somewhere in that it seemed like if I could get Thad to choose me, it would make everything all right again."

"But it didn't?"

"I thought it had at first. It felt as if it had. I started to think that being married to Thad was what I'd wanted all along, that I just hadn't realized it. I was happy. Content, even. For a while. Then these really awful feelings started to surface all by themselves. Sometimes Thad would tell people that I hadn't wanted him until someone else had and it would make me so mad I'd just feel like I was going to explode. I'd find myself looking at him and seething at the thought that he'd played me against someone else. That he'd put me in that position. The image of him with Adele would pop into my head and stab me all over again, and—"

Chloe sighed and shrugged, not really wanting to get any deeper into it. "I finally had to admit to myself that what Thad had done had damaged what I'd felt about him even though I was late in realizing it. It had damaged our relationship. And that things couldn't just go back to the way they'd been so we could live happily ever after."

"So you didn't go through with the wedding."

Chloe shook her head. "No, I called it off and moved out of Thad's house."

"And that was really it? The end of the back-and-forth?"

"That was really it. Thad accused me of getting together with him again only so I could leave him, so I could say I was the one to end it and nobody could think he'd left me for someone else when that was what he wished he had done, he wished he had stayed with Adele. It was ugly."

"Did Thad go back to Adele?"

"I don't know. I haven't seen or heard from him since. Not even when my folks were killed a month later. We didn't have any real mutual friends, and without my mother running into his mother, there hasn't been a grapevine. I do know that if he *did* get back with Adele after leaving her for me, she'll probably have a lot of the same hard feelings. But who knows, maybe she would be better at shaking them off than I was and things could work out for them."

"You'd be okay with that?"

"I would be. Now. I can't say that I didn't go through a rough patch after Thad and I called it quits. That I didn't grieve and miss him and still have a few weak moments when I'd think maybe I'd made a mistake. Especially after my parents died, when I was feeling pretty alone. But I got past that and finally saw that even though I really did care about him, if he was the one for me I would have known it long before eight years and I wouldn't have needed so many breaks from him. So, yes, no matter who he ends up with, I wish him well."

Reid nodded.

"And there you have it," Chloe concluded. "The gory details you wanted. Not nearly as entertaining as the home movies were."

That made him smile and seemed to break the tension that had come from talking about Thad. For them both.

Reid eased into a grin and said, "I'd forgotten about some of the stuff in the movies. I'd forgotten about your beauty marks."

Chloe laughed. She had three moles on her shoulder that Reid had used to draw a gargoyle face when she'd dozed off while lying in the sun at his house one Fourth of July. When she'd woken up she hadn't noticed his artwork and until she did, the joke was on her with him and the rest of his family. The whole thing had been caught on film, including her surprise when she'd realized what he'd done and her retribution. Aided by his sister, Cassie, Chloe had filled water balloons with a mixture of pancake syrup, food coloring and stinky cabbage juice. When Reid least expected it they'd bombarded him and drenched him in the disgusting concoction.

"I'd forgotten about my revenge until I saw that," Chloe said as if she were still savoring it.

"What about the beauty marks? Do you still have them?" he asked.

"I do. I've been told I should have a dermatologist check them out to see if they should be removed, but I've never done it."

"Can I see them?"

Chloe arched an eyebrow at him. "Is that the doctor talking or have your come-ons gotten that bad?"

He laughed. "It's the doctor in me talking. I was just thinking that you kept the gown on for the post-accident exam so I didn't see the moles. Maybe I should take a look at them. We can just slip your sweater off your shoulder."

"Oh, sure, that's what they all say," she joked.

She didn't see any reason not to comply, though, so she did push the wide neckline off one shoulder, exposing the three black dots.

And then she saw the reason *not* to have done it.

Because when Reid leaned forward to take a closer look—a very close look since the light was so bad— she remembered what had come with his apology for drawing on her. He'd said he was sorry later that Fourth of July night when they'd been alone, assuring her that he loved her moles and proving it by kissing each one. Separately. Slowly. Softly…

Chloe could tell he was thinking about the same thing suddenly. There was something in the almost minute change in his expression, in the fact that after a moment of looking at the marks, he raised his chin as if he might be going to kiss them again.

Chloe held her breath, wanting him to do it and knowing she shouldn't be wanting it. Knowing he shouldn't do it.

But he didn't.

"They look okay to me," he decreed, rearing back and replacing her sweater.

Only when he did that, his hand came into contact with her shoulder.

And stayed.

Chloe didn't have the impression that it was intentional, that he actually had used the beauty marks as a ploy. She honestly had the sense that once that accidental contact had been made, he simply didn't have the willpower to break it. And neither did she.

It was just that his hand was big and strong and warm and there it was with the ball of her shoulder fitted into his palm, and it felt astonishingly good.

They both raised their gazes from his hand on her at the same time, meeting eye to eye.

But he didn't take his hand away.

And she didn't tell him to.

She definitely didn't tell him to, even though she tried to persuade herself that that was what she needed to do. No, instead she laid her own hand to the side of his ruggedly masculine face.

Chloe couldn't be sure who kissed who then, whether Reid had leaned in to her or she'd gone up to him or if they'd met in the middle. But before she knew either of them had moved at all, Reid's mouth was over hers and it was as if that kiss she hadn't wanted to end the night before could finally go on the way it was meant to.

And go on it did.

Reid's hand at her shoulder did an enticing but brief

massage before trailing up her neck to the back of her head. He weaved his fingers into her hair and gently offered support as he deepened their kiss.

His other arm came around her and he pulled her closer just as his lips parted and Chloe's lips answered in kind, not hesitating even a split second when his tongue came to reacquaint itself with hers.

He'd been good at that before and he didn't disappoint now. Confident and playful, he toyed with her, tempted her and ultimately rewarded her with a sexy twist that titillated more than she expected.

Chloe's hand fell from his cheek to his chest where those pectorals that looked hard and honed lived up to their appearance. Muscular, toned—whatever sports he was playing with the Northbridge Bruisers had paid off because he felt so amazing beneath her palm that she doubled her pleasure by placing the other one there, too.

Mouths opened wider still and tongues waged a sensual battle and somehow they were no longer sitting against that carpet roll, they were lying beside it.

Chloe's hands traveled to Reid's shoulders, to his hair, around to his back, splaying themselves against that expanse and bringing her nearer to him, making her suddenly very aware of the awakening of her breasts, which seemed to reach out to him on their own.

Her nipples were crying for more than to merely brush against his chest, glorious though it was. They made themselves known by turning into tight little knots that Chloe thought he must be able to feel through her sweater and the simple strapless tube top she wore underneath it.

Maybe that was why his kiss became more urgent, more demanding, why his tongue darted and thrust in and out at hers in a simulation of what was beginning to be on Chloe's mind, too.

It was her hands that relayed her own rapidly growing needs, beginning with a fevered massage of his back, first on the outside of his T-shirt and then slipping inside it, kneading with fingers that stopped just short of digging into him.

One of his legs came over hers then, pulling her even closer against him, the hard ridge of his body doing some nudging, too.

And that wasn't the only one of Chloe's leads he followed. While his mouth still plundered hers, his hands found the hem of her sweater, going under and up, pausing when he found tube top rather than bare breast but making quick work of pulling it down. Once he had, he captured an engorged, straining globe with a hand that felt so amazing Chloe couldn't keep from moaning, from arching her back and filling his palm with even more of her.

Not that any help was required. The man had incredible hands that molded and stroked, squeezed and caressed, tickled and teased, pulled and circled and tormented her until her nipples were diamonds of delight strung to that center of her between her legs with an ever-tightening cord. That ever-tightening cord that he strummed, making her writhe against him.

Gone was his mouth from hers then, kissing, nibbling, trailing down as one of his hands raised her sweater and exposed her breasts to the cooler air of the room.

But the chill didn't last long before Reid took first one breast and then the other into that ardent mouth of his, sucking, nipping, tracing her nipple with the tip of his tongue, drawing her deeply in only to release her and start all over again.

There was artistry in his hands, his fingers, his mouth, his tongue and teeth, and she was soft and pliable, sensitive and susceptible to his every touch, every caress, to every movement.

He was taking her to a point of no return and she knew it. But she also knew that she had a decision to make. Knew that she had to decide whether to go that far or not.

Oh, how she wanted to!

Her body was crying out for her to.

And maybe she would.

Maybe she would...

"This is not just friends," she heard herself say, unaware of where it had come from.

"Is that what we're supposed to be? Just friends?" Reid asked between flicks of his tongue against the very crest of her right nipple.

"I don't know..." Chloe nearly groaned. "I don't know what we are...."

Reid slowed what he was doing, running only the tip of his nose around that same nipple before he stopped completely.

"I don't know what we are either," he confessed in a voice that was so raspy it was almost guttural.

"I'm afraid of complicating what's already—"

"Not simple," he finished for her.

"Definitely not simple," Chloe said in a whisper.

Reid braced his weight on one elbow, pulling her sweater down with his other hand while being very careful not to touch her.

"So you don't think this is a good idea?" he asked, making it an understatement and tinting it with humor.

Chloe rolled to her back, putting even that slight distance between them, and closing her eyes. "I'm trying really, really hard to convince myself it isn't a good idea."

Reid chuckled and ran a single index finger along the side of her face. "Yeah, me, too."

"But it probably isn't a good idea, right?" she asked.

"Probably isn't," he agreed but there was no mistaking the reluctance in it.

She heard him sigh and roll to lie flat on his back beside her, breaking all connections so that their bodies were no longer touching anywhere.

That was how they remained for a few minutes. Chloe didn't know for sure, but she thought Reid was getting himself under control because that was what she was doing.

Then she heard him move again and she opened her eyes to watch him get to his feet.

He held out a hand to her. "Come on. I have to get out of here before wisdom doesn't prevail."

Chloe took his hand—warm and strong and leathery—and remembered all too well how wonderful it had felt on more private parts of her anatomy. Wishing much too much that it was still on those other parts…

But she merely got to her feet, too aware of her still-taut nipples against the inside of her sweater now that her tube top was around her waist.

Reid let go of her hand and retrieved his jacket, slinging it over one shoulder rather than putting it on. Most likely because he was as overheated as Chloe was and didn't need it to go out into the night.

She tagged along with him to the front door where he said, "I need to do some things at my mom's tomorrow so I won't be here."

"Not at all?"

Too disappointed. She shouldn't have said that.

"No, not at all. But tomorrow night… Will you keep it open for me if I don't tell you why?"

Chloe laughed a little. "That's very mysterious."

Reid gave her a devil's smile and wiggled one eyebrow. "That's me—man of mystery. Will you do it?"

She wasn't going to see him during the day. The thought of not seeing him in the evening either was more than she could tolerate.

The best she could do was pretend indifference. And she *was* only pretending.

"I don't think my calendar for tomorrow night has been filled yet so I suppose I could keep it open. But I hope you know I wouldn't do it for just anyone."

She'd been trying for a joke but he grinned as if he'd taken it seriously and it pleased him to hear.

"I'll bring clothes," he said then.

"You'll bring clothes?"

"I'll bring clothes," he merely repeated, adding to the mystery and clearly enjoying himself in the process.

"You should probably wear clothes," she said, baffled by this conversation.

"Don't ruin things," he chided, still teasing. "Do your hair and…whatever…the way you would if you were going somewhere special, and just put on sweats or something easy to change out of when I get here."

"You're going to dress me?"

He closed his eyes as if he were in rhapsody. "Don't tempt me," he said with a sigh before opening his eyes again and smiling down at her once more. "Probably I'll let you do that on your own. I'll just supply the clothes."

He leaned over then and kissed her again, his free hand combing through her hair in back for a second time, his mouth open and his tongue making one final, roguish parry before he ended the kiss and straightened up.

But his hand remained where it was, holding her face up to his while he peered into her eyes for a long moment before he finally said, "Tomorrow night," in a tone Chloe wasn't sure what to make of.

Then he took his hand away and used it to open the door and let himself out.

Leaving Chloe with a body still pulsating with all that he'd aroused in her.

And that was when she stopped denying that the chemistry that had supercharged their young romance wasn't as potent as ever.

That was when she stopped telling herself that she had any more power to resist it—or Reid—than she'd had fourteen years ago.

And that was when she finally admitted that while she didn't know where this might end up, she and Reid would never be just friends.

Chapter Ten

"You're late," Reid said in greeting to Luke when his brother finally got to their family home at noon on Friday.

"I know, I'm sorry," Luke answered, taking off his coat and hanging it on the hall tree in the entryway before coming into the living room.

"Where is everybody?" he asked Reid.

"The girls are all at the beauty shop, and Joshua, Ad and Ben are out at the bridge."

"And we're supposed to bring up the folding chairs, make room for them in here and rearrange the dining room for the buffet, right?" Luke said.

"Those are the instructions I've been left with," Reid confirmed.

"Shall we drag the chairs out of the basement first?"

"Sure." As they headed for the basement, Reid said, "What made you late again?"

"We finally got through to the first FBI agent who handled the bank robbery," Luke explained. "He left the bureau a few months after it all happened, went to work for the CIA and retired from there a few years ago so it took some work locating him. We're still waiting for the files from the whole investigation, but since we managed to track this guy down I wanted to be in on the conference call to hear what he remembered about the part he did handle. I just got off the phone not ten minutes ago."

"Did you learn anything worthwhile?"

"Everything is a piece of the puzzle," Luke said philosophically. "This guy followed a lead that the reverend's wife and one of the two farmhands were in Canada. From Canada he trailed them to Alaska, but everywhere he went they'd left just ahead of him. From Alaska he went to Seattle and caught Frank Dorian—"

"Frank Dorian," Reid repeated while they both grabbed as many folding chairs as they could carry. "He's the guy whose blood type you haven't been able to find to make sure the blood on the duffel bag was the other robber's—"

"Yeah. We already know Mickey Rider's type—the other robber. We still don't have Dorian's blood type for comparison, but what we *do* have is some information from the old FBI guy about his questioning of Dorian."

They'd taken the chairs upstairs. While they retraced their steps for a second load, Luke filled Reid in.

"Frank Dorian swore he and Rider went separate ways from Northbridge, that he didn't know where Rider had gone or what he'd done from there."

"So no confession to killing Rider and stuffing his belongings in the rafters of the bridge."

"No. But after extensive questioning Dorian broke and admitted to the bank robbery—although he claimed his share of the money was all spent. And since we know none of it was ever recovered, it's anybody's guess if that was true or not."

"What about the reverend's wife?" Reid asked. "Where was she?"

"I think I told you there were bets about whether Celeste was with Dorian or Rider. Turns out whoever's money was on Dorian won—he'd had the affair with her. But he said he'd ditched her in Alaska," Luke said.

"But if Dorian killed the other robber he might have done harm to the reverend's wife, too," Reid postulated.

"Definitely a possibility. But the story he told was that he'd gotten fed up with Celeste. This all took place about five months after the robbery and he said that she couldn't get over the guilt of having abandoned her kids, that she cried all the time, that she didn't care how she looked—she was gaining weight, not bathing, going days without combing her hair—and since that was all unappealing to him and the fun they'd had when they were here was over—"

"He just left her?" Reid concluded.

"That's what he said—that one night after she'd cried herself to sleep, he slipped out."

Reid grimaced at the idea. "I guess if someone leaves her husband and kids for a bank robber she can't really rely on that bank robber to be an upstanding, reliable guy, but geez, you have to kind of feel bad for the reverend's wife."

"I'm thinking that if all Dorian did was leave her to fend for herself in Alaska, she came out ahead," Luke countered.

They'd brought up all the folding chairs and they began to work on the living room furniture, each of them taking an end of the sofa to move it from its position in the center of the room to the wall in front of the picture window.

"Did the former FBI guy think Celeste was in on the robbery? That she might have the money?" Reid asked in the process.

"Dorian said that he and Mickey Rider had pulled the bank job on their own, that Celeste had no idea they were going to do it and hadn't had any part in the robbery itself. The FBI guy believed him, said Dorian had been pretty convincing. There wasn't any evidence either way to that point, which was where he handed the case over to other agents and left. His work for the CIA took him out of the country then, so he didn't keep up with where the investigation went from there and couldn't tell us anything else."

Once the last of the folding chairs were opened and placed around the perimeter of the living room, they moved on to the dining room. Taking opposite ends of the oval table they lifted it to the back wall of the room, then enlarged it by adding the extension leaves.

"Where do you go from here?" Reid asked, referring to the bank robbery.

"Now we wait for the files the FBI is still trying to dig up and send. We need to see what's in them, and why there's no record of Dorian going to trial after he was in custody."

"That's right—there would be a public record of that if it had happened," Reid said.

"And there isn't. Until this guy told us on the phone that he'd nabbed Dorian we'd had no idea that anyone connected to this had ever been caught."

"So this was a fairly big piece of the puzzle."

"It was something, anyway. If you figure we're getting our information in bits and pieces, this was a piece, not a bit, but there are a whole lot of questions still unanswered," Luke said. "From 1960 till now is a long time for a case to cool off."

They began to take the dining room chairs into the living room to add more seating there.

"And speaking of cooling off," Luke said as they did. "It looked like you could have used a little when you finally got home last night."

You'll never know how much, Reid thought.

But he wouldn't admit it. Instead he said, "Me? Nah."

"Sure, uh-huh…" Luke countered dubiously just as the doorbell rang.

"Here we go. That should be the cake or the caterer," Reid said, glad for the interruption so his brother couldn't go further into the subject of Chloe.

"I'll let them in while you make space in the fridge for the trays," Luke said.

But Reid hadn't taken more than two steps when his brother's voice stopped him.

"Just be careful, Reid. Don't forget that on Monday when we close on the house Chloe will have cut all ties with Northbridge. I'd hate to see her leave town with your heart on a stick for the second time."

"Older and wiser, little brother. I'm older and wiser," Reid said, sounding confident.

But the confident tone aside, he was just hoping that he *was* wiser as he headed for the kitchen.

Because the night before he hadn't felt old or wise. Not when he'd wanted Chloe more fiercely than he'd wanted her fourteen years ago.

So fiercely that he'd actually gone home wondering why he couldn't have her.

Which was something he was still wondering, even after reminding himself all night and all morning of the fact that had Chloe felt about him the way he'd felt about her all those years ago their past might have played out very differently.

But this wasn't the past, Reid thought. This was the present. And it was possible—likely—that they were at the same level when it came to whatever it was that was going on between them now.

They were attracted to each other. Sure he was hotter than hell for her, but he felt reasonably certain that she was as hot for him or things wouldn't have gone as far as they had the previous evening. But beyond that? Neither of them knew what was beyond that except that, as Chloe had said, they weren't *just friends*.

So if this wasn't the past, if they were something

more than mere friends and they shared a mutual attraction that wasn't any more or less on one side or the other, why *couldn't* they explore whatever it was that was going on right now?

Damned if he knew why they couldn't, he concluded as he opened the refrigerator to survey the situation inside.

But he wasn't too focused on the contents as his mind continued on the course that had been absorbing him since he'd left Chloe last night.

He just couldn't make himself believe that they couldn't explore what was happening between them now as long as he was aware that Chloe was leaving. As long as he didn't let himself forget that, he thought he could keep his perspective. Keep himself from being blindsided the way he had been years ago. He could be careful—as his brother had advised.

Caution was a good thing.

But it didn't necessarily mean he couldn't proceed.

"Proceed with caution," he muttered as he moved a few things in the refrigerator to make space.

But definitely proceed.

Proceed without pinning any kind of hopes on any kind of eventual outcome. Proceed without expecting anything but whatever happened in the moment. Proceed with his eyes open. But proceed.

And maybe come out of this with another good memory of Chloe to wipe away the bad ones he'd been left with. Maybe just enjoy himself. And her. And being with her again. Maybe just enjoy wherever that went without worrying so much about it all.

Why not? he asked himself.

No reason why not, he decided.

He wasn't a lovestruck kid anymore. He wasn't in any deeper than Chloe was. He didn't think he had anything to lose.

So Luke had been right about him being careful—he'd give him that. But his brother was wrong otherwise.

There was just no way Chloe could leave town again with his heart on a stick.

Not if they would have made love the night before, and not if they made love any other night, either....

"You brought me a dress?" Chloe said that evening when Reid showed up at her door, bearing a black sweater dress, a package of thigh-high nylons and a pair of three-inch-heel mules.

"The dress is a loaner from Alyssa Cantrell—everyone agreed the two of you were the closest in size. The shoes are Cassie's—she said they might be a little snug but you could probably make do. And the hose are new—Mom picked them up for you this afternoon."

Chloe stepped out of the way so he could come inside, still having no clue what was going on.

"You look nice," she said, searching for a hint in the fact that he was wearing a black suit that couldn't possibly have been tailored by Northbridge's dry cleaner—where any suit purchased in town was altered.

In fact, unless something drastic had changed in the small town, a suit like Reid was wearing couldn't have been bought there. It looked Italian; it hung from his broad shoulders and hugged his narrow waist as if it had been made specifically for him, and he looked a whole lot better than just nice. He looked applause-worthy standing in her living room in that suit and a canary-yellow shirt and matching tie.

Chloe tried to get past the mind-numbing effects of his appearance, though; she leaned forward and whispered, "What's going on?"

Reid mimicked her actions and answered, "I can only tell you now because it's too late for word to leak out and the press to get wind of it and ruin it—Cassie is marrying Joshua Cantrell. In about half an hour."

"Ah," Chloe said as she finally understood. "*That's* why they came into town under cover. And last night must have been the rehearsal dinner."

"Yep. You wouldn't believe the things reporters and photographers do to get to them. Or what they have to do to avoid them. I don't know how Cassie puts up with it, but she says it's all worth it to be with Joshua so I take her word for it. They're both hoping that once they're married and Joshua isn't on the list of hot-property available bachelors anymore they'll be let out of the limelight. But for now, this had to be done under the strictest secrecy."

"I never guessed," Chloe assured him.

"But now that you know, the question is—will you go?"

She would have gone just to be with Reid. This only made it all the more intriguing. "I'm honored to be included," she said, which was true, too.

Reid handed her the clothes. "I knew you wouldn't

have packed anything to wear to something like this—
that's why the makeshift wardrobe."

Chloe reined in her excitement and, as if going to a
hush-hush celebrity wedding was something she did
every day, she said, "I'll be as quick as I can," before
hurrying upstairs to change.

The dress was a simple, very short, straight-up-and-
down slinky little number. It had long sleeves and a
fold-over neckline that was off the shoulder. Chloe fell
in love with it the minute she got it on.

The shoes were another matter—they pinched a bit.
But since she didn't have another option she had to wear
them.

She hadn't really taken Reid's instructions from the
previous evening too seriously but now that she knew
where she was going she added another layer of mascara and a touch more blush, and she made sure to use
the lipstick she'd forgotten to apply at all until then.

She was glad she'd shampooed the attic dust out of
her hair when she'd showered earlier, and after another
brushing, some scrunching and a few flips upside down,
she left it to cascade around her naked shoulders.

Then she did one final check in the full-length mirror—mainly to make sure that the dress camouflaged
the fact that she hadn't been able to wear a bra under
it. But the fold-over neckline accomplished that and
once she was certain of it she returned to the living
room and Reid, who devoured her with his eyes before
a grin of appreciation slowly spread across his face.

"Holy moley," he said as if the wind had been
knocked out of him.

Chloe laughed. "*Holy moley?* Who says that?"

"Anybody looking at you in that dress."

"It's a good dress, isn't it? Cashmere."

"It's a good dress on you."

Chloe couldn't suppress a smile at the compliment and the fact that he seemed genuinely awestruck.

But she recalled that he'd said they had only half an hour and so she didn't think they should waste any time.

"Shouldn't we go?" she asked.

It took him a moment to answer but he finally emerged from his admiration to agree. "We should."

Chloe held up the dress coat she'd brought downstairs with her. "Believe it or not, I found this in the attic. There were a lot of winter things up there that we didn't take with us to Arizona. Most of them I'm giving to charity, but I was going to take this back with me for the occasional cold snap."

Reid took the coat from her and helped her into it. "This is great because the wedding is outside. Sort of."

"In your mother's backyard?" Chloe asked as they headed for the door.

"The reception will be at the house. But the wedding is at the bridge."

Reid's SUV was in her driveway when they left the house and she waited until they were situated in it to repeat what he'd said.

"The wedding is at the bridge?"

"I'm not completely clear why, but as near as any of us can tell, Cassie and Joshua had a date or something out there, and that's where they wanted to get married.

There will be heaters and candles and lights for warmth, but I still think you'll probably be glad for the coat." He started the engine but before he backed out of the drive he cast her another smile—this one wicked—and said, "Not that I'd hate it if you needed me to keep you warm."

The image of his arms wrapped around her, holding her close to him, was too appealing to entertain at that moment so Chloe fought it by getting back to the subject of the wedding.

"With everything that's going on about the bank robbery and the reverend's wife and that duffel bag that was found out there, I would have thought the bridge was a crime scene or something," she said.

"It was off-limits for a couple of weeks while Luke and the rest of the cop force went over it. But they didn't find anything else and finally decided that after all these years there probably wasn't anything else to find. They let the reconstruction work get underway again and that's been more an issue for the wedding than anything. But Ad, Ben and Joshua were out there today while it was being decorated and Ad says no one will even be able to tell there's work still being done on it. I do have information about the robbery, though," he added.

"The latest scoop?"

"The very latest—fresh in today."

"What is it?"

Reid filled her in, complete with the robber's claim that he'd left Celeste in Alaska and why.

"That's so sad," Chloe said when he'd finished. "I mean, yes, it's awful that the reverend's wife deserted him and her own two sons. But then to regret it and not be able to go back? And on top of it, have the man she thought she loved write her off just because she wasn't pretty enough or fun enough anymore? To have him sneak out on her in the middle of the night, leaving her in a strange place, knowing no one? You have to feel a little sorry for her."

"Yeah, I thought so, too," Reid agreed as he turned onto the road that led to the bridge. "Maybe I shouldn't have told you tonight and wrecked your festive mood."

"No, it's okay. I suppose it could be argued that she got what she deserved. But you do have to wonder what happened to her after that."

"Not tonight we don't," Reid decreed. "Tonight we only have to go to a wedding."

They'd reached the bridge by then and it was difficult to think about anything else when it came into sight.

It was an old covered bridge that looked as if it belonged somewhere in Vermont or Maine rather than Montana. Its lower half was solid wood planks, its upper half a crosshatch latticework, and while its roof was only at the tar paper stage, it was hardly noticeable because the whole bridge was aglow with tiny white lights.

"Oh, this is beautiful," Chloe said as Reid parked beside the other cars already there.

White candles lined both sides of the approach to the bridge as if it were the aisle of a church, and the opening was wreathed in vines of yellow and white roses. Warm golden light flooded from the interior, beckoning to the family and few friends who were filing onto the bridge.

Reid got out of the SUV and came around to open Chloe's door, offering her a hand to help her out.

She took it without thinking about it and while she knew she probably shouldn't have, while she knew she probably shouldn't let him keep hold of it either, it was still wonderful to walk up that candle-lined drive with him that way as strains of classical music played by a string quartet greeted them.

Under the bridge's cover, more white lights, roses and candles turned the simple structure into a cathedral. White folding chairs provided seating that faced a platform where the ceremony would be performed. Rows were divided into four chairs on each side of a pale yellow runner down which the bride would walk, and Reid led Chloe to the vacant first row.

"I'm one of the groomsmen so I'll leave you here and meet up with you again after the ceremony. It won't be long and once Mom and Ben give Cassie away they'll sit with you."

Chloe nodded her understanding and took the third chair from the center as Reid disappeared behind the white curtain that formed a backdrop to the platform.

She didn't have long to wait before the wedding began. The quartet segued from an adagio into the Wedding March and everyone stood, turning to the end of the bridge from which they'd all entered.

Cassie's sisters-in-law were her bridesmaids, dressed in long butter-yellow satin chemise dresses and carrying bouquets of baby's breath and white rosebuds.

Cassie followed, with her mother on one arm and her twin brother, Ben, on the other.

All eyes were on the bride's entrance as she approached and only when she reached the platform did Chloe face that way again and see that the minister, the groom, Ad and Reid had slipped out from behind the curtain.

When Lotty Walker and Ben were asked to, they handed Cassie over to Joshua Cantrell and both joined Chloe in the front row, whispering hellos before all attention turned to the ceremony itself.

Well, not *all* attention, because Chloe's attention was focused far more on Reid than it was on the words being said.

Tall, straight, clean-shaven, combed, pressed and perfect. She was struck again by the man he'd grown into. By his strong, confident bearing. By how staggeringly gorgeous he was.

But she was struck suddenly by something else, too. She was proud of him, she realized. Proud of what he'd become, of what he'd made of himself.

She was also inordinately happy to be there with him and it didn't have anything to do with the past. In any time, any place, she realized, she would have been glad to be with him, to be seen with him, to be the one he chose to share an occasion like this with.

And for once she didn't counter that feeling with any reminders of anything.

She merely sat there and basked in it, and in the beauty that was around her, in the sense of satisfaction that being there with Reid gave her.

Chapter Eleven

"There's my favorite great-nephew and his lovely wife, Dee. See? I remembered."

Chloe had gone with Reid to bring a plate of food to his great-aunt just after the wedding reception had begun. He'd warned Chloe that his seventy-five-year-old aunt had dementia but that greeting seemed to have a ring of truth to it. Even if Chloe was not someone named Dee.

"No, Aunt Bernie, this isn't Dee. This is Chloe Carmichael. If you think back, you might recall the Carmichaels, they used to live here in town. Chloe owns the house across the street from Luke and me. We're buying it as a rental."

"Chloe Carmichael?" the older woman exclaimed, squinting at Chloe through thick-lensed glasses. "Is she that girl you were in trouble with?"

Reid cast Chloe an apologetic glance. "That was a long, long time ago, Aunt Bernie. There's no trouble now."

He adeptly got his aunt to focus on the food they'd brought her and then excused them so they could get something to eat, too.

But Chloe's mind wasn't on the mouthwatering array of catered delicacies that adorned the dining room table when she and Reid returned to it.

He had said he'd been curious about her post-him love life when they'd talked about it the previous evening. Chloe had been more in the mindset of not thinking about his, of keeping him frozen in time and pretending he hadn't had a love life since she'd left Northbridge.

But now there it was, glaring at her, and she couldn't ignore it. She had to know if what the older woman had said could possibly be true. So the moment they had filled plates of their own she said, "Let's find a quiet spot where we can talk alone."

"We could hide on the basement steps for a while."

Chloe couldn't tell whether or not he knew what was coming, but if he did, he didn't appear reluctant and she accepted his suggestion.

"Great, let's go there," she said, heading in the direction of the door that concealed the stairs.

It wasn't a quick trip as they were drawn into chats on the way through the crowd but they finally made it, slipping through the basement door and closing it behind them.

The old wooden stairs that led down into the unfinished, cinder-block-walled clutter weren't fancy but they did offer some privacy. Chloe and Reid went about four steps down before sitting at facing angles so they could see each other.

But Chloe didn't wait until she'd tasted any of her food to say, "Your wife, Dee?"

Reid grimaced, took a bite of a mini-brioche topped by olive and red pepper tapenade, and then said, "I didn't think you had missed that."

"Was it the dementia talking or was it—*is* it—true?"

"It's true that I *did* have a wife. Dee. Dee Fellows. But it *isn't* true anymore."

Married. Reid had been *married.*

To someone other than me...

It just wouldn't sink in.

"You were *married?*" Chloe said, sounding as shocked as she felt.

"I was."

"And you didn't say anything? Even last night when I went on and on about Thad?"

Reid nodded toward her plate. "Eat and I'll tell you all about it."

The last thing Chloe wanted was food. Or to be put off. "Tell me," she said quietly.

"There didn't seem like an opening last night or any other good time to bring it up before that, so I didn't say anything."

"It's been brought up now."

"So it seems. And now you want to hear about it."

Now she *had* to hear about it.

"All the gory details," she said, repeating the phrase he'd used to urge her to tell him about her love life.

He didn't rush into the explanation, however. It took him a moment before he sighed resignedly and said, "Okay. Dee Fellows..."

He paused again, staring at the stairwell wall for so long that Chloe began to think he was having second thoughts about letting her in on this at all.

"Please," she said as if pleading to be let out of some misery he was causing her.

His eyebrows arched but he conceded, glancing at her again. "After Tucson I came back here and pretty much hit bottom. I did a lot of drinking. A lot of picking fights. A lot of acting like a big man. And in that vein of proving what a man I was... Well, I rebounded."

"You rebound by dating someone, not by *marrying* someone."

"Yeah, well. That would have been a better way to go. But that's not what I did. I married someone. Dee suffered an appendicitis attack on a road trip through here late that summer. She had to have emergency surgery and be admitted to the hospital. I was working there by then—when I wasn't hungover or being a jerk."

"You met and fell in love over a bedpan?"

Oh, that was crass and crude and uncalled for! Chloe knew it the minute the words came out but she was feeling so many things she couldn't get a handle on, that it had been pure reaction.

Reid seemed to take it in stride, though.

"I don't recall any bedpan action, no," he answered, even smiling a tiny bit, as if he understood what was happening to her as she heard this. "But Dee looked a little like you, she had the same coloring, and, I don't know, there was something about her that appealed to me—like I said, it was a rebound thing and I was a long way from being in my right mind after you'd dumped me."

Knowing she'd had a part in pushing him into someone else's arms didn't help.

Chloe moved her plate from her lap to the step above them just to keep from looking at Reid for a moment.

Then she shored her defenses to hear more and said, "Okay. Go on."

"I visited with Dee, I helped her take the walks up and down the corridor that she was supposed to take, things like that, but enough that by the time she was released we'd started up. She didn't want it to end there by going back home to Milwaukee so she came up with a plan. Her father was supporting her and she convinced him that she should stay here to recuperate while her friends went on without her, that while she was here she'd check out the college. In reality, she didn't have any intention of going to school, but she thought it was an excuse her parents would buy and get behind. She was right. They gave permission for her to rent a room at the bed-and-breakfast and the way was paved for us to be together."

It was so difficult to hear this. How had he stood it the night before?

But Chloe was still compelled to know the entire story. "You started to date," she said to encourage him to continue.

"And I rushed into a relationship with her that shouldn't have gone beyond that. I've analyzed it to death, Chloe, and the thing is, I thought I'd stepped up to the plate with you and the baby, that I'd done what I should have done, that I'd been a man about the whole thing. Then I'd been treated like some inconsequential kid. When Dee happened… Well, dating again, proposing, taking it all the way to marriage, let the world know I really was an adult. It gave me back a sense of power. Of control. It proved I was the man I'd thought I was with you. Even though it was probably the most immature, irrational thing I've ever done, at the time, that's how I saw it."

Jealousy was still eating Chloe alive, but she also once again felt bad for Reid, for what he'd been through fourteen years ago, and she suffered a renewed twinge of guilt for the part she'd contributed.

But before she could say any of that Reid continued.

"Anyway, it was a huge mistake. Dee was from a wealthy family. She'd lived a spoiled, pampered life and all of a sudden she was married to a small-town boy working his way through college. She wanted me to quit school altogether. She wanted us to move to Milwaukee where her father owned a chain of appliance stores. She wanted me to go to work for him. She wanted the ladies-who-lunch kind of life her mother had—not that she'd had any different kind of life herself up to then because she'd never worked a day."

"And none of what she wanted was what you wanted."

"No, it wasn't. There was no way I was quitting school and moving to Milwaukee to sell refrigerators for my father-in-law. Not only was that something I didn't want to do, there was the whole pride issue again.

I wasn't taking a handout job and money from her family, moving to where they lived and letting them tell me what to do. By then I'd taken a big turn from the hell-raising of that summer before I met Dee and I knew I wanted to not only stick with college, but go to medical school. That meant hitting the books hard to make sure my grades were high while still working as many hours as I possibly could at the hospital to support us and to pay tuition and save for med school. It meant years more of education, internship, residency, struggle—"

"Especially if she didn't work."

"And if I didn't take financial help from her family, which I refused to do. So she ended up bored and disappointed. Angry. Petulant. And I was tired and impatient and…" Reid shrugged. "It was just all wrong and in the end Dee was hurt and I knew none of it had been fair to her because the truth was, I still had it bad for you. We were divorced before anniversary number two."

But there had still been nearly two years when he'd been someone else's husband. When he'd had a wife. When he'd been part of a bona fide couple with someone other than her. Reid and Dee…

"I just… It's so strange to think of you that way."

Reid didn't seem to have an answer to that so he merely nodded.

"And what about since your…divorce?" Chloe asked, finding it odd to say that, too. To think that he'd been through a *divorce.* "You haven't been married three or four times, have you?" she added, thinking that almost anything seemed possible now.

"No, just the one time. Since then I've dated but there hasn't been anything serious. I guess you could say that after you *and* Dee, I've been gun-shy myself."

The basement door opened just then and Ad poked his head in. "There you are. We've been looking for you two and somebody said they saw you come through here. Cassie and Joshua want the groomsmen in some pictures, Reid."

"Yeah. Okay. Give us a minute, will you?"

Ad retreated and closed the door again, and Chloe was assaulted with more bizarre thoughts.

Someone else had been Ad, Ben, Luke and Cassie's sister-in-law. Someone else had been Lotty's daughter-in-law. Someone else had joined and belonged to the Walker family in the spot Chloe had pictured herself....

For the second time she felt like an outsider.

And she didn't like it. A lot.

It must have shown on her face because Reid said, "Are you okay?"

"It's all kind of tough to take," she admitted.

"Don't I know it," he commiserated.

But it was also her own fault, Chloe told herself. She'd told him in Tucson that they were through. He'd been fair game. A free agent.

But even knowing that didn't make her feel any better.

"We should go up," she said anyway because she couldn't simply keep him there on the stairs, all to herself, the way she was suddenly inclined to do.

"Maybe you can eat while I take pictures," he said, nodding towards her still-untouched food.

"Sure," she agreed just to appease him because food had no appeal to her right then.

"Come on," Reid said, getting to his feet with his own plate of barely eaten wedding supper.

He held out his hand to her as he had earlier and Chloe again took it, marveling at how that simple contact, that simple connection, the familiarity of it, could make her feel a little better. But it did and she didn't want to let go.

She had to, though, as she picked up her own plate and they headed for the door to rejoin the celebration.

But even when she was back with everyone, drinking champagne, talking and laughing again, she still couldn't help thinking about the fact that without ever realizing it consciously, she had always considered Reid to be hers.

And now she knew that wasn't the case.

That he had belonged—truly belonged—to someone else.

That he could—and likely would—belong to someone other than her in the future.

And that she didn't like the idea of sharing him.

Not at all...

It was after 1:00 a.m. when the wedding reception ended and the last of the guests left. Joshua Cantrell had hired a crew to come in and clean up the next day, so the Walkers were spared that chore and merely said the last of the congratulations and welcome-to-the-families, and filed out, too.

After the ceremony at the bridge, Reid had parked

his car in his own driveway and he and Chloe had walked to his mother's house. As a result—like the night before—they needed to walk home again. Luke wasn't along tonight because he'd taken the bride and groom to Billings where they were to leave on their honeymoon, so once everyone had driven off, Chloe and Reid were alone on the block.

Unlike the previous evening, though, tonight Chloe was wearing torture chambers on her feet and once the coast was clear, she paused to take them off.

"I just can't go another step in these," she explained.

"You'll get frostbite on this cold sidewalk," Reid said.

"Not even that could hurt as much," Chloe declared.

But once she straightened up with shoes in hand, he surprised her by whisking her up into his arms.

Chloe gasped and grasped him around the neck to hang on while the four glasses of champagne she'd imbibed gave her the whirlies.

"You can't carry me!" she insisted even as he did just that and began walking again.

"I think I can," he claimed, not showing any signs of hardship as he crossed the street to the side her house was on.

Chloe thought she should probably protest until he put her down but it was fun and she was tipsy and instead she just hung on and enjoyed not only the ride but the chance to study his face up close. His beautifully masculine face…

Reid cast her a quizzical glance. "What are you doing?"

"Looking at you," she said simply.

"Like what you see?"

"You're not hard on the eyes, all grown-up," she answered, making him smile a small smile.

But he didn't dwell on the compliment or the attention. He changed the subject. "If you don't count the talk we had on the basement stairs, did you have a good time tonight?"

"I did, but it's impossible *not* to count the talk we had on the basement stairs." And now that she was thinking about it again—and more relaxed thanks to the liquor—she said, "Can I ask you a question?"

"Sure."

"Over the years did you—somewhere in the back of your mind or something—think of me as yours?"

"No."

"No?" she repeated forlornly, not only surprised and disappointed by the answer itself, but also by the lack of thought he needed to put into it.

"No," he confirmed.

"Oh."

"Thinking that you *weren't* mine was part of the torture after Tucson. I imagined that you'd found somebody else. That you were seeing a bunch of other guys, that you'd moved on completely and that that's why you hadn't wanted any part of me. Having to come to grips with the fact that you *weren't* mine was what made it all the tougher." He glanced at her again with a hint of smugness in the smile that let her know he'd had his fair share to drink, too. "Why? Is that how you thought of me? As yours?"

They'd reached her house as he asked that question

and that spared her from answering it because he leaned over to provide her with access to unlock and open the door rather than placing her back on her feet to do it, and that was what they bantered back and forth about. Then he carried her across the threshold and once they were inside kicked the door closed behind them.

But he still didn't put her down. And he clearly hadn't forgotten what they'd been talking about prior to the pause because he said, "Well? I'm not setting you free until you answer me—did you always think of me as yours? Is that why the whole Dee thing came as such a shock?"

"You were *married*," Chloe said, still hedging. "That's pretty shocking."

"Especially if you've always thought of me as yours," he said, barely containing another smile that reflected how much he liked this revelation. He jiggled her. "So have you?"

"You aren't going to be able to carry me around forever," she pointed out, again not admitting anything.

"Maybe I should try a different tack then," he suggested, setting her on her feet and backing her against the closed door.

He pushed her coat down her arms to her elbows, then dropped a kiss on one of her shoulders.

"Maybe I should try something like this," he said on his way to kissing the other shoulder.

Chloe smiled at the honeyed sensation of his mouth on her bare skin. "Oh, that *is* agony," she said facetiously. "It'll make me blab for sure."

"Say it," he ordered, kissing the side of her neck.

"Say that even when you were with *Thad* you thought of me as yours more than you thought of him as yours."

"I've always heard that doctors have big egos," she said, letting her head fall against the door and freeing the way for him to kiss the hollow of her throat.

"I didn't bring this up, you did," he reminded.

"And if I say it? Then what happens?"

"I don't know. Maybe for tonight I'll *be* yours," he said as if he were reciting a line from a cheesy movie.

Chloe laughed. "Oh, whatta guy! Thank you so much."

"We've already established that we aren't just friends," he pointed out.

"And that you're someone's *ex-husband*," she countered as if that were a deal-breaker.

If he had a comeback for that he didn't bother with it. He was too busy kissing a line from the hollow of her throat to the neckline of the dress she was wearing.

Soft, tender kisses. Some of them accompanied by tiny flicks of his tongue against her skin that left just a little dampness that tingled dry when exposed to air. This set off more of the tingling all through her, tightening her nipples and doing a fluttery dance in the pit of her stomach.

What had they been talking about?

Ah, yes…that he was someone's ex-husband….

But somehow that suddenly didn't seem very real. This was Reid. *Her* Reid. Older and better—so much better—but still her Reid. Her Reid no matter what…

He made a U-turn at the folded top of the sweater dress and found the ridge of her collarbone with more kisses. Kisses that were little shockwaves of delight, rippling all the way to her fingertips, to her toes, to secret places in her center.

Reid might have belonged to someone else but he was here with her now.

Kissing her now.

Belonging to her again now.

And suddenly that was the most important thing.

That and how good those kisses felt...especially when they finally reached her mouth.

Warm, supple lips covered hers, slow and sensual and sweet with enticement. And Chloe realized in that instant that every bit of what he'd aroused in her the previous evening was still thriving, springing back to life with renewed vigor fed by each and every kiss.

She'd wanted him the night before and she wanted him now. And nothing she'd learned about him in the past few hours had changed that. She just wanted this moment with the man who she now knew had had a place in her heart since the day she'd met him.

His lips parted and Chloe answered them and invited more by raising her hands to his shoulders, to his neck, to the back of his head, massaging, testing the short bristles of his hair.

In some ways he'd always been hers and she'd always been his—whether he'd realized it or not. In some ways they always would belong to each other. And after having this week, after sorting through all their history, after discovering that there still was something between them, Chloe just couldn't deny herself this. Not tonight.

Reid cut short their kiss suddenly, moving to her earlobe to nibble that before he said, "Don't get me to where I was last night and pull the plug. I don't think I can live through it again."

She didn't think she could either. And she knew she didn't have the will to try. Tonight she didn't have any willpower at all. Or the inclination to drum up any.

The only inclination she had was to let go of everything and just give herself over to him.

So her answer was to sneak both hands under his impeccable suit coat and take it off his shoulders to toss aside.

Reid got the message. He chuckled and yanked his tie free, throwing it with more enthusiasm to join the jacket.

He recaptured her mouth vigorously as he unfastened his collar button. But that was the last of the attention he paid to his own clothes. While his lips opened wider and his tongue came to conquer hers, he took her coat off the rest of the way and sent it to become part of the pile of discards.

Once he'd done that, his hands went to her shoulders, cupping them, squeezing them, reminding her of what they'd done to her breasts the previous evening and turning her nipples into sapphires of longing.

Opening her mouth, too, and letting her tongue be a little bold, Chloe reached up to the remaining buttons of his shirt. She unfastened them, pulling his shirttails free to finish the job, exposing only a strip of his pectorals and rock-hard stomach—but for just a split second before her greed to have his chest and torso completely bare overcame her, and off went his shirt.

When it was gone, she left no inch cheated. Raising her flattened palms from the breadth of his back she brought them to his shoulders, to his biceps, delving into the toned muscles of powerful arms, traveling to the solid, steel-hard mounds of his pecs, to male nibs that grew taut beneath her touch. She even let her hands go to his flat, flat belly and below where she unhooked the waistband of his pants.

But that was as far as she went with that and the return of her hands to his back elicited a groan of complaint as his mouth and tongue plundered hers and his own hands did a slow slide down her arms, taking her dress lower and lower.

He began the trail of kisses again then, pushing her dress below one breast to find it with his mouth as he pressed it upward with one hand cupping the lower orb.

Chloe was more than ready for that, craving, yearning for his touch, for the feel of his mouth, his tongue, his teeth there. Her head rested against the door again as he sent the tubular sweater dress on a descent that took it completely below both engorged, straining breasts, baring them to the cooler air of the room.

But that cooler air reminded her that they *were* in the living room. With the undraped picture window just feet away.

"Anybody can see in," she managed to whisper even as her breath caught on the deep draw of her sensitive flesh into the hot, moist cavern of his mouth.

Reid retreated slightly, taking one nipple just between his lips in a brief, velvety kiss before moving away completely.

Holding her hand, he headed for the stairs.

Chloe used her other hand to pull the dress high enough to conceal breasts that felt as if they might burst for want of more of his magic, impatient to be where he could go on with what he'd only begun at the door.

Reid took her into her bedroom, beside her bed. He didn't hesitate to shove the dress completely down then, letting it fall to her feet where Chloe kicked it aside and stood before him in nothing but thigh-high hose and bikini panties.

"Now you," she ordered with a glance at his pants where the zipper bulged with promise.

He took something from his pocket first and threw it onto the bed. Then down went the well-tailored slacks, along with whatever he'd had on underneath them and shoes and socks, too.

Leaving Reid naked.

And Chloe literally breathless with the magnitude of what she feasted her eyes on. There was absolutely no boy left in him. He was all man. Incredible man...

"Ohhh..."

He laughed a confident laugh and placed a small, tender kiss to her crown.

But looking alone was not something he was going to leave her to. He ran his hand down her arm, caught her hand and brought it to that long, iron-hard proof that he wanted her as intensely as she wanted him.

Then he eased them both to the bed, kissing her again—a profoundly sensual kiss—before he shed her nylons and panties and then rediscovered her breasts with a deft hand that held them to his seeking mouth.

And while Chloe had been enjoying the exploration of the man he was now, he began to set free so many things inside her that she couldn't hold on; she lost herself in all that he was doing to her.

Kneading, massaging, molding her breasts, each in turn. Urging them upward to a mouth that drew her into that warm wetness she'd longed for more of. To a tongue that circled her nipple, flicked the crest, nipped and tugged and tortured her with pleasures.

Then his hand sluiced down her stomach to her hip, to her thigh, and up the inside of it to that spot between her legs that was waiting none-too-patiently for him.

She couldn't keep from writhing slightly when he initially reached her. When talented fingers entered and retreated and drew ever-so-tantalizingly forward. Her spine arched and raised her from the mattress, twisting her to her side, to face him.

On its own her hand reached him again, renewing what she'd begun earlier, caressing him, exploring him, reveling in the silk-over-steel shaft that seemed to burgeon within her grasp. To strain for her the way every part of her was straining for him.

After one more intense draw of her breast into his mouth, he abandoned it, rolling to his back for a moment to use the protection he'd tossed onto the mattress earlier.

Then he returned and with both of them on their sides, he pulled Chloe close, raising her leg over his hip and finding his way inside her with more than his fingers. So much more. Inching into her until he filled her with the glory of his amazing body, using his hands to bring her nearer, to hold her to him as he started to move.

Small, almost circular movements of his hips at first. Then in and out oh-so-slowly, so carefully, so adeptly. A divine prelude. A primer that merely prepared her for the coming attraction. That heightened her anticipation. That awakened every nerve ending, every sense, attuning her to him so that when he took that first, firm thrust into her, she welcomed it, she craved it, she needed it.

She met it and held him deep within her for one lengthy moment before releasing him and then accepting him back again.

And again. And again. Faster. Deeper. Harder.

Clinging to him, Chloe met and matched him, striving, straining, working to form what felt like a glistening, rainbow-hued crystal inside her. Bright and shining and growing bigger and bigger with each meeting, each retraction, with each coming together of their bodies. Until that crystal had expanded beyond containment.

And when it had, it exploded into a million tiny, bright, brilliant pieces of platinum glitter that rained all through her and held her in a blinding silvery glow for one moment out of time that she wanted to go on and on and on....

And she thought it could have when Reid rolled her to her back, their bodies still melded together, plunging home himself. His arms pushed his upper half away from her, his lower half even closer to the core of her as his own climax grabbed on to the end of hers and took hers with it to a second and whole new level of exquisite, unrivaled, passionate triumph more acute than anything she'd ever experienced.

Then it ebbed for them both.

In tiny increments that brought Reid down to her again—chest to breasts, cheek to cheek, hips to hips as her pounding heart settled to a normal beat and her labored breathing relaxed beneath the lovely weight of his big body.

She heard him take in a breath of his own, full and deep, exhaling it in one final, replete release.

Then he turned his face from the mattress to her and kissed her ear.

"Worlds have collided," he whispered.

"Yours and mine?"

"I think so. Have you survived it?"

"I think so," she echoed with a small laugh. "How about you?"

"Survived and then some," he said.

After another moment of stillness, he rolled them both to their sides again, holding her to him as he did so that their bodies stayed joined. Then, when he had her where he seemed to want her—cocooned in his arms, his leg over and hooked around hers—he looked down at her and smoothed her hair away from her face with one gentle, caring hand.

He kissed her forehead before delving into her eyes with his again.

"Don't tell me to go home," he commanded.

Chloe smiled. "I won't."

"But I need to sleep."

"Me, too."

"Like this," he said, pulsing inside her.

It felt so good it was almost enough to start her up again and she tightened her muscles around him in response.

"Like this," she confirmed in a bare whisper, letting her head come forward to rest against him.

"Like this," he repeated, his voice groggy and yet sounding a little turned on again, too.

Then, in a tone that was wicked and seemed to pledge more, he added, "For just a while."

"Okay," she agreed with a laugh.

The grogginess seemed to win out, though, because Chloe felt him relax all around her.

So she gave in to her own fatigue and closed her eyes.

But she didn't fall asleep instantly. For a time she just reveled in the stillness. In the quiet. In the warmth of Reid's body. In the feel of his steady, even breathing into her hair.

And all the while she kept trying to pretend that she didn't feel as if she were finally where she was supposed to be....

Chapter Twelve

"Reid! I thought you were across the street working on Chloe's house and here you are, sleeping. At two in the afternoon. Are you sick or something?"

Luke's voice woke Reid but he'd been so deeply asleep that it took him a moment to wake up. To realize that he was at home, on his own bed but not under the sheet or blanket. That he was fully dressed in the jeans and T-shirt he'd put on early this morning when he'd come from Chloe's to raid his own refrigerator for eggs and bacon—the food he'd served Chloe in bed when he'd gone back.

He sat up and swung his legs over the side of the mattress, rubbing his face roughly.

"Hey," he said thickly in answer to his brother who was standing in the doorway.

"Are you sick?" Luke repeated.

Only then did Reid recall that his brother had asked the question before.

"No, I'm fine. Terrific, in fact." Except that he needed about four more hours of sleep.

"When you weren't home this morning I figured you'd gone over to work early. So if you aren't sick, what're you doing here sleeping?"

Reid couldn't help smiling. Grinning, probably.

And apparently that gave Luke an indication of what had gone on across the street after the wedding, because he said, "Tell me you didn't."

"All I'll say is that I was across the street, but no, I wasn't working." Or sleeping much since he and Chloe had barely napped between multiple rounds of love-making—one that had followed breakfast this morning before they'd finally agreed that if he stayed there, neither of them would ever get up today.

So he'd come home, dropped onto his bed and nearly passed out.

"Oh, man…" Luke groaned as if what he was assuming Reid had done across the street didn't sit well with him.

"Did you need something?" Reid asked, still slightly dazed and wondering why his brother had been looking for him at all.

"I told you I had to work this morning but I thought I could get out this afternoon to help you over at the house. But the FBI files on the bank robbery came in so I'm going to have to go back to the office instead."

"Okay."

"I'm not sure anything is okay," Luke countered,

sounding a tinge disgusted and even more concerned. "Are you sure you know what you're doing?"

"Right now I'm just trying to wake up," Reid said.

"Because you were with Chloe all night and didn't get any sleep," Luke concluded as if he needed it spelled out for him.

"It was a great night," Reid said with awe edging his own voice.

"Yeah, well. As I was coming in here a minute ago it looked like the rental company was delivering Chloe a replacement car for the one she wrecked on her way into town Sunday night. Let's just hope you didn't hang too much on that great night only to watch her use the new car to leave you high and dry again."

"Was she loading her suitcase or something?"

"That woke you up, didn't it? No, she wasn't loading her suitcase or anything else. She was just signing a clipboard. And now that I think about it, she'd probably been sleeping, too, because she was in clothes that looked like they'd just been thrown on and her hair didn't exactly look combed." Luke paused. Then he said, "Don't get me wrong—I like Chloe. I'd like to see things work out for the two of you if that's what you want. But what I *don't* need to see is you going through what you went through before. You said you were older and wiser but what I'm wondering is just how wise it was to spend the night with her."

"It'll be fine," Reid said.

"I'll keep my fingers crossed that you're right," Luke countered with a worried frown. "Anyway, I have to get to the office and dig into those files."

"Sure, go ahead. I'll probably still get some work done on the house today."

"Why am I not optimistic about that?" Luke said under his breath.

Reid glared at him, silently warning him that he was overstepping his bounds.

Luke shook his head, sighed, and said, "Not that it does much good at this point, but seriously, keep your guard up, will you?"

"Everything is under control," Reid assured.

Luke's expression was skeptical but he only said, "Talk to you later."

"Later," Reid answered.

He waited until he heard Luke go downstairs. Then he got up and went directly to the window.

Reid's bedroom faced the street so he could see Chloe's house. There was no sign of her or of whoever had delivered the replacement, but there was a car in the driveway that hadn't been there before. And it had a sticker on the bumper that advertised the rental agency.

So Chloe had wheels.

It was surprisingly unsettling to Reid.

Yes, he'd known the car would be coming. That Chloe was only in Northbridge temporarily. He just hadn't been thinking about the end of her time here. And after the way they'd spent the last dozen or so hours, he didn't *want* to think about it.

But with the car right under his nose and the closing on the house only a day and a half away, it suddenly struck him that he'd better think about it.

He moved from the window and headed for his

shower, trying to put his thoughts in order as he went into the connecting bathroom and shed the clothes he'd thrown on when the only thing on his mind had been getting back to Chloe.

It was tough for that not to be the only thing on his mind now—getting back to her. Seeing her. Touching her. Kissing her. Making love to her. Being with her every minute that he could be…

"Oh, man…" he muttered to himself. "If that isn't shades of the past, nothing is."

Undressed, he turned on the water and got into the shower, adjusting the temperature and then standing underneath the spray, eyes closed, letting it rain over him as his own words echoed in his head.

Shades of the past…

Okay, yeah, some of what was happening with Chloe was a lot like what had gone on when they were an item long ago, he conceded.

Long ago, through good times and bad, Chloe had been the first thing he'd thought about when he woke up every morning.

Long ago, images of her had crept into his head a million times a day.

Long ago he'd watched for her from up the street, from down school corridors; he'd been attuned to the sound of her voice, to any mention of her name, to even the scent of her skin.

Long ago, a little rush had gone through him every time he'd seen her. He'd planned his days, his nights, his weekends around her. He'd done everything he could to be with her every minute he could be.

And all of that was true now, too, he admitted as he thought about it. As he thought about working in her house and listening for sounds of her upstairs, hints of where she was, what she was doing. As he thought about the thrill, the satisfaction, that had gone through him whenever she'd finally come down from the attic. As he thought about how he'd planned most of the last week around her—before and after settling things between them. How he'd taken into consideration when he should get to work across the street so he didn't disturb her. How he'd gone for coffee so he could bring her a wake-up cup each morning. How he'd put off his lunch most days in hopes that she might come down for hers and give him an excuse to eat with her.

He'd wanted to be with her. Plain and simple. Some of the time even when he hadn't been particularly happy with her, he'd still had a drive to see her—just like in the past. And once he'd gotten happy with her again? Then the drive had been even stronger.

That was all a lot like the way he'd felt as her teenage boyfriend.

And then there was last night…

Last night had been off the charts.

Last night was a night he wanted every night to be.

Pretty much the way he'd wanted every night to be like the night they'd made love for the first time all those years ago.

He stepped out from under the spray of the shower and grabbed the bar of soap, working up a lather.

As he did, he also recalled that while *he* had wanted every minute, every night, with Chloe, she hadn't felt that way. Okay, sure, when they were dating she had. But after the pregnancy? When he'd been willing to jump through any hoop to have her still, she certainly hadn't felt the same. And he knew he couldn't ignore that.

He'd believed after their breakup—and had thought again when they'd discussed it all the other night—that Chloe hadn't had the same feelings for him that he'd had for her. But thinking about that now, about Chloe's point of view fourteen years ago and about the night they'd just spent together, he began to wonder if it was true that he'd cared more about her than she had about him.

What if the difference hadn't been in their feelings for each other? What if the difference had been in their responses to the situation they'd found themselves in?

Every time they'd talked about the past Chloe had let him know that she'd cared about him, that she'd wanted to be with him, that she'd missed him, but that regardless of how she'd felt, she'd done what she'd thought was best for them both. Hell, she'd cared enough to protect him from the threats her parents had made against him both here and in Tucson—that wasn't a sign that he hadn't meant anything to her.

But they *had* both been kids. And no kids were prepared for a pregnancy. His reaction had been that whole prove-he-was-a-man thing that had gotten him into trouble later on with Dee. But Chloe's reaction had been something else, and for the first time Reid thought about it with some objectivity.

He thought about Chloe not as the girl who hadn't lived up to his youthful expectations of her, but as simply a girl. Like girls he'd had as patients. Teenage pregnancy patients.

Chloe had been on the verge of hysteria when she'd discovered she was pregnant and he'd figured that he could calm her fears by taking charge. But now he realized that taking charge probably hadn't had a lot of effect. Not when no matter how much of a tough guy he'd been, she'd still been the one facing a *pregnancy*. Facing giving birth and caring for a child.

And there were her parents—no small hill to climb there. Not for Chloe. He'd known his mother would help and support him no matter what. But Chloe's parents were a whole other story. Stern, intimidating, harsh, obsessed with appearances and social status and reputations—definitely not the kind of folks to get behind a pregnant teenage daughter. As he'd discovered for himself when he'd tried to convince them to.

So it was no wonder that Chloe hadn't had a simple vision of their predicament as just a premature beginning to the plans they'd already had in mind for themselves. No wonder she'd been—had to be—more practical. More realistic.

And really, she'd had a point when she'd said that had they gotten married, had they ended up teenage parents, he likely wouldn't have become a doctor, and she might not have even finished high school, let alone gone to college. Not to mention the possibility that the marriage might not have survived. So it *couldn't* honestly be said that they weren't both better off the way things had turned out. Only Chloe had seen that in advance, while it took hindsight for that to become clear to him.

But now that it was clear to him, now that he thought about it all again with that perspective, it occurred to him that neither his response nor hers had been based solely on how they felt about each other. Sure, his had seemed to have more roots in that, but if he were honest about it, he knew his reaction had had as much to do with proving himself and making sure everyone knew he was willing to do the right thing, as it had had to do with loving Chloe and wanting to be with her for the rest of his life.

So maybe despite loving him, Chloe had made her own decisions on the more pragmatic way she'd viewed the situation. Not because she'd cared for him less.

That actually made sense to him, he thought as he shampooed his hair.

But what about now? he asked himself.

It was the present that had Luke worried.

But then Luke hadn't been in on all the times Reid had been alone with Chloe. He certainly hadn't been in on last night, Reid thought as he stepped back under the water to rinse off soap suds and shampoo lather.

But what about the times they'd been alone this past week? What about last night? Were there indications of Chloe's thoughts and feelings in them? Were there signs that in spite of what his brother might be worried about, he didn't need to be?

It seemed to him that there were.

Sure, at first Chloe hadn't been gung-ho about spending any time with him. She'd been hesitant. And why wouldn't she have been when he'd been such a jerk to her in the emergency room right off the bat?

But once he'd mellowed and overcome her resistance, Chloe hadn't balked at any of the suggestions he'd made that had them spending time together. She'd gone with him to whatever he'd invited her to. She hadn't begged off sharing meals with him. She hadn't given him the impression that she was eager to have him say good-night and leave.

And when it came to last night? He hadn't had to twist her arm. In fact, he'd given her the opening to say no. To send him home. And she hadn't taken it.

No, she'd been as much into making love as he had. She'd even initiated a few things herself as the hours had gone on, and this morning she'd lured him back to bed when he'd figured on having breakfast with her and getting to work. None of which seemed to point to someone who felt differently about him than he felt about her.

So if the situation fourteen years ago had caused their actions more than unequal feelings for each other, and if their attraction—and maybe feelings—for each other now were pretty even, was it such a stretch to think there might be something between them again? Something good? Something worth working at? Something that could pan out? Maybe even pan out the way they'd thought it would in their adolescent frenzy for each other?

Why not? he asked himself.

Especially now, when it seemed as if the slate was clean and he was finally seeing their past realistically.

Why not, when he wanted Chloe? When there weren't any obstacles and they actually could have a future together?

Why the hell not…?

He didn't have an answer for why not because he honestly thought there was a real chance for them now. In fact, he thought that maybe the reason everything had happened in the past, the reason they'd been swept apart, was because it had been the wrong time. For them both.

But now seemed like the right time. The perfect time. The time when everything could finally fall into place the way it was meant to.

Because if any two people were meant to be together, he and Chloe were those two people.

And he believed the odds were good that Chloe knew it, too. That that was why she'd let them spend the night before making love. Getting as close as they had.

"Could be you can stop worrying, Luke," Reid said as if his brother were within hearing distance.

Then he turned off the shower and grabbed his towel in a hurry.

Because now that he was convinced he'd worked everything out in his mind, he was itching to work it out for real.

Chloe was in the kitchen measuring grounds into the coffeemaker when she heard the front door open. She didn't have to look to know it was Reid coming in.

It made her smile and filled her with a warmth that she savored while he made his way through the living room and into the kitchen to join her.

And not only did he join her, he came to stand

directly behind her, wrapping his arms around her waist and pulling her back against him before he'd said a word.

Only after nuzzling her nape with his nose did he poke his chin over her shoulder in direction of the coffeemaker and say, "I could use a cup of that."

Then he kissed the side of her neck where it was bare above the crew-neck T-shirt she'd put on with jeans when she'd gotten out of the shower a scant half hour earlier.

"Hmm…" she mused, savoring every bit of that moment—of having him there again, of the feel of being in his arms, of the heat of his breath on her skin, of the playfully intimate rapport that was once more between them. "Someone might think you didn't get much sleep last night."

"That's because *someone* kept me awake all night slaking her insatiable needs."

Chloe laughed as she poured water into the machine, replaced the pot and turned it on. "*Slaking* my needs? What is *slaking?*"

He nibbled her earlobe. "Want me to show you while the coffee brews?"

"Maybe…" she said, amazed by the fact that she just couldn't seem to get enough of him.

"Nah," he countered. "First I want to talk."

Chloe laughed again, thinking he must be joking. "Yeah, right. You want to talk," she said facetiously.

Reid uncircled his arms from around her waist, took her shoulders in both hands and turned her to face him. "I mean it. I want to talk first."

He was smiling so Chloe still didn't take him too seriously. She merely shrugged and said, "Okay. Talk."

His hands went to her sides and he lifted her to sit on the section of countertop that hadn't been removed yet, reaching around to move the coffeemaker closer to the wall so it didn't burn her and then resting his hands loosely on either side of her hips.

"I saw the rental car," he said then.

"They just delivered it. That's what dragged me out of bed or I'd probably still be sleeping."

"It got me to thinking."

"The rental car?"

"Mmm-hmm. About you leaving town again."

That seemed like a more sobering subject than his approach had led her to believe. At least it was a more sobering subject for her. And one she was trying not to think about.

"We still have today and tomorrow," she pointed out. "I decided to stay for the closing and called Betty to tell her I'd be there. And I can wait until Tuesday morning to drive back to Billings to catch a plane."

"Not enough. Which is what got me to thinking," he repeated. "Last night was—"

"I know," Chloe said because it had been so astonishing for her that there were no words that could do it justice.

"It was the way I want every night to be," he finished anyway. "That's what I realized when I saw the car and that's what gave my mind a jump-start."

He went on to outline in great detail the entire thought process he'd gone through, from reminding her of all he'd believed and resented for so many years, to the fact that even when she'd explained everything to him on Wednesday night he'd still gone home believing that his feelings for her had been greater than hers for him, to his sudden change in perspective just since her replacement rental car had arrived.

"…and what I realized when I finally made myself see it that way, was that everything you did—and didn't do—was because of the circumstances," he concluded. "So there isn't any reason we can't pick up where we left off and still have a future together."

Chloe hadn't had any idea where he was headed when he'd initiated this conversation. But through the course of what he'd said, her own spirits began a decline that hit rock bottom with that final declaration, and she felt her eyes go hot and wet with tears.

But not tears of joy.

She didn't know where she'd thought things between them might go from here. She'd had her own hopes. Hopes that maybe clearing up Reid's misconceptions about what had happened fourteen years ago was enough to wipe away his resentment and anger, his hard feelings. Hopes that maybe something honestly could work out for them.

But listening to him, to what he'd said, to what he'd thought, to the fact that nothing at all had been wiped away until the last hour or so when he'd started to think about her leaving town, seemed to her to have a deeper message in it. A message she couldn't overlook.

"So when we talked the other night and you made that crack about my being level-headed and you being a hopeless romantic—that wasn't really a joke, was it?

That was still how you saw it all—you saw yourself as a hopeless romantic because you were sure that you cared more than I did."

"Yeah, but now—"

"And when I asked you if you could let go of everything you'd hung on to for so long—all the awful feelings—because you finally knew what went on on my side and you said you could? That wasn't true if you went on believing that if I'd had the same feelings for you, I would have come back."

"It was true for the most part. I was accepting that it was just a fact of life that our feelings hadn't been the same. And acceptance has its own benefits. One of them being that it's freeing, that you can let go of some of the lousy feelings."

Chloe looked at him and wanted so badly to think something other than what she was thinking. Because there he was, his face a masculine masterpiece, his green eyes penetrating and intelligent, his body magnificent and something hers was craving in spite of what was going on, and her heart actually seemed swollen with all she felt for him.

But she couldn't help thinking that it was obvious that what he was experiencing was something she was familiar with. That same need, desire, drive she'd gone through with Thad. That need, desire and drive that had absolutely nothing to do with sex.

She shook her head, closing her eyes to keep from crying and only opening them again when some of the sting was gone.

"I thought… I was hoping…" she began haltingly,

her voice soft and cracked. "Maybe I was just kidding myself, because I know even after we talked Wednesday night I was worried that you weren't being completely honest with me. And I told myself not to forget all the bad you'd felt for so many years, that that was still under the surface. But then things between us just got better and better, and I guess I let myself start to believe that it was okay. That it would *be* okay—"

"You're losing me, Chloe," Reid warned, frowning at her now as it seemed to be sinking in that this was not going the way he wanted it to.

"You're doing what I did with Thad," she said bluntly, cutting to the chase.

"I'm still lost."

"I told you, I thought getting him back would fix everything. It would make all the bad feelings disappear. And they did for a while. But those bad feelings leave scars—really deep scars. You can't get rid of them. They stick around under the surface and choose their moment to come out again."

Reid's frown deepened and he took a turn at shaking his head. "What are you saying? That I only want us to get together now to make up for the misery I went through? To compensate? That it's some kind of subconscious need for payback? So once I have you where I want you, I can dump you to even the score?"

"No, I know you're not trying to even the score. I told you that was what Thad accused me of and that wasn't the case, so I know it isn't the case with you either. It's just that you think you can go back, that you can erase those fourteen years of ugly thoughts and feelings, turn back the clock and pretend nothing ever happened. Thad could do that because he wasn't the one who had been hurt. I think I could do it now, with you, because I haven't resented you and been mad at you all this time. But you have resented me and you have been mad at me. And that's what I'm saying—I saw how you felt about me on Sunday night when I came into the emergency room. Fourteen years later, Reid, and you could hardly stand the sight of me. And Monday morning when you came to call a truce? It was so begrudging—"

"But that's changed—"

"After fourteen years of it? As far as I know, you might even blame your failed marriage and divorce on me since you said that came out of the things you ended up feeling and thinking when I never came back. That's a lot of baggage carried around for a very long time."

"And I just told you I've resolved it all."

"No, what you just told me was that you talked yourself out of what you've carried around for your entire adult life. That you talked yourself *into* believing you're fine with everything suddenly. Which is what I did with Thad. But that isn't the same as honestly being rid of the baggage or the scars left by carrying it around. And in the end, I think those are the *real* feelings."

"Our situation and your deal with Thad aren't the same," Reid insisted. "You found out your fiancé was cheating on you, that he'd betrayed you. That he'd rejected you. What happened with us was out of our control and I was stupid to think all this time that there was anything you could have done about it. Or anything you *should* have done differently since you were right—we *were* just kids, we needed to grow up, to get our educations. You may not have been able to forgive that other guy, but there's nothing I *need* to forgive. I see now that what played out fourteen years ago was the way it should have played out. And it's over. *Long* over. Anything going on now is only on your part…"

Something seemed to occur to him and he backed away from her. Completely away, into the center of the kitchen, looking at her suddenly as if he were seeing something he hadn't seen a moment before.

"That isn't it, is it? This isn't about my scars and hard feelings and the dumb things I've carried around with me forever. This is about how you feel about me again. About your not wanting us to have a future together now, either—"

"No—"

"Yes, it is. I was wrong. This past week… Last night… I thought there was more to it all for you because there was more to it all for me, but there wasn't. Last night you might have been hot for me, but that's all there was to it. I read more into it and—" He shook his head again, this time disgustedly. "We're right back where we were—"

"No," Chloe insisted. "You're wrong."

"Really?" he challenged. "Then you want us to put the past to rest once and for all? You want us to go on and have a future together?"

He'd never know how much she wanted that. Badly enough for those tears to be back in her eyes again, hotter and fuller than before.

But now she knew for sure what she'd only suspected before—that he'd been holding on to his hard feelings despite telling her that he could let them go. And she didn't—couldn't—believe that standing before her was a man free of the kind of scars that would haunt and tinge any relationship they ever tried to have.

"I wish—more than you'll ever know—" she said, losing the battle with her tears and feeling them running down her face. "I wish I could say I thought we could have a future together. But I know we can't."

"Because this is just like fourteen years ago—I'm more invested than you are. Again. I can't believe it!" he said, throwing his hands in the air, turning his back on her.

"No, you're not!" she shouted and sobbed at once. "But look at you—no matter what you say, no matter what I've said this week, you go on believing that you cared more than I did all those years ago, holding it against me, ready to jump to the same conclusion again. What kind of future would we have together with that always there and ready to pop out, Reid? Would we have a future where I hoped you had forgiven me even though we both know you haven't? A future where your real feelings come out again to punish me and eat at you and make us both miserable if you spend more on my Christmas gift than I spend on yours, or if you make a bigger deal about something I do than I make about something you do? Because that's what I see for a future together—constant questioning, constant insecurities, constant looking for inequalities that deep down you'll always be convinced exist between the way I feel about you and the way you feel about me."

"Forget it," he said through clenched teeth, his voice a knife stab. "What's the saying? Fool me once, shame on you. Fool me twice, shame on me. Well, shame the hell on me."

And then, without casting her so much as a glance over his shoulder, he walked out of the kitchen and out of the house, slamming the front door behind him.

Leaving Chloe still sitting on the countertop.

For a few minutes she stared after him, not thinking that he would come back, not even knowing why she was looking into that empty room, at that closed door.

Then what had just happened really hit her.

Her head dropped below her shoulders and the tears dripped onto her thighs.

And for the life of her she couldn't figure out how something that seemed so good between two people could turn out so badly.

Twice.

Chapter Thirteen

Chloe spent the rest of Saturday afternoon and all evening alone in the house, wishing she hadn't already told the Realtor she would be in town for the closing on Monday, and regretting that she hadn't paid any amount of money to have the attic debris shipped to her so she wouldn't have had to come to Northbridge at all.

So when her old friend Sugar called on Sunday morning and invited her to the farm, Chloe didn't hesitate to accept.

She spent until two o'clock finishing the work on the attic and loading the rental car with boxes she could take to the post office on her way out of town the minute the closing was over. Then, grateful that she wouldn't have to be faced with hours and hours more of being drawn to stare at Reid's house across the street, she headed for the countryside.

She drove out of Northbridge proper and into the farm- and ranchland that stretched from the south of town. It was a bright and brilliant autumn day. There wasn't a cloud in the sky; the air was crisp and clear. She passed several properties decorated with pumpkins, squash and other multicolored gourds. Others were adorned with dried cornstalks bundled together around fence posts. One showed the season change with orange and gold and red leaves strung on vines and used as garland along rails, and another got into the spirit of Halloween with work clothes stuffed and made into scarecrows positioned on either side of the gateway that led to the house and barn.

Had she not been in abject misery, her eyes raw from no sleep and almost nonstop crying since Reid had left her the day before, Chloe would have enjoyed the drive and the festive scenery. As it was, she just worked at keeping any more of the tears at bay and hoped Sugar wouldn't notice the telltale evidence.

Sugar lived in the house her husband's family had passed down through three generations—a two-story farmhouse at the end of a long drive that led from the main road. It was painted a cheery yellow and trimmed in white, and Sugar came out the front door to meet her as she pulled to a stop in front of it.

Chloe waved and turned off the engine.

Sugar waved back but Chloe could tell from the sympathetic expression on the other woman's face that Sugar had already heard that Chloe and Reid had parted ways again.

"I made Hank take the kids into town to his mother's and told him to stay until I call and say he can come home so we can have the place to ourselves. I didn't think you'd be in any mood for my husband and noisy sons," Sugar said after greeting Chloe, hooking one arm through hers and escorting her inside.

"You didn't have to do that."

"Men and boys—the last thing you need in your face right now are those. After more Reid drama I figured an all-girls time was called for."

"More Reid drama?" Chloe echoed, marveling at the speed of the small-town grapevine. "What makes you think there has been more Reid drama?"

"Church this morning. Reid didn't come and it was his Sunday to bring his mom. Luke was with her instead and when I joked that you must be keeping Reid busy, he told me things had gone down the tubes with the two of you again."

Chloe nodded and fought the intense urge to ask what else might have been said about Reid, about what he was doing and saying and feeling and thinking now.

In aid of the fight she said, "Show me your house."

Sugar did, not pressing the subject of Chloe's falling-out with Reid. In fact, Sugar didn't even get into it when they'd finished the grand tour and settled in the living room with a plate of cranberry-walnut scones and cups of tea. Instead she said, "I have the latest about the reverend's wife and the bank robbers."

"The last I heard was that one of the robbers had been caught by the FBI but no one knew why he hadn't gone to trial, that he'd left Celeste in Alaska and swore that she didn't have anything to do with the robbery. Have you heard anything since that?"

"I have a friend who works at the newspaper and this is what will be out tomorrow—I guess the FBI files finally got here and the reason the one robber never went to trial is that he tried to escape and was killed in the attempt. Plus, apparently when Celeste was tracked to her last known location in Alaska, the FBI was told that she was coming back here. That she was determined to get back to Northbridge and her kids no matter what."

"I did hear that she regretted leaving her kids."

"The report on the Alaska investigation said that she more than regretted it," Sugar elaborated. "She was obsessed with seeing them again so there was no doubt she would do whatever she could to get back. The FBI contacted the cop here—I guess there was only one then and there was something about him being only a temporary guy or maybe somebody who just didn't work out, I'm not sure which. Anyway, the FBI notified him to keep his eyes open for Celeste because they were so sure she'd show up."

"Did she?" Chloe asked, laughing a little at her friend's enthusiasm, and marveling again at the speed of the small-town gossip mill and grapevine.

Sugar shrugged as if whether or not Celeste Perry had returned to Northbridge was the question of the century. "The guy they told left right after that and all he did was write a little note somewhere about it, as if it wasn't any big deal. So when the new guy took over he either didn't see the note or didn't think it was important and didn't bother with it. The note to keep an eye open for Celeste was the last mention of anything to do with the robbery and now our guys are considering the possibility that Celeste actually might have come back to Northbridge somehow. It sounds like they're going to start investigating here. Can you imagine? What if she's been in Northbridge or somewhere nearby all this time?"

Chloe just couldn't get as excited as Sugar seemed to be. Although she wasn't sure what could excite her in her current state of mind. But she didn't want to seem disinterested, so she said, "It doesn't seem possible that anyone who had lived in Northbridge could come back here and stay without being recognized."

"But still, what if was true?"

Obviously Sugar was intrigued by the idea and Chloe didn't want to ruin it for her, so she merely said, "I keep hearing about how sorry the reverend's wife was that she left here, that she abandoned her kids. I have to feel sort of sorry for someone who must have felt as if she made one wrong turn in her life and then paid so dearly for it."

"That's true. When you look at it like that, you do have to feel kind of sad for her. We all make mistakes."

"Not usually as big as deserting kids to run off with bank robbers, but, yes, we all do."

That seemed to put an end to the conversation as Sugar got up from where she was sitting on a rocking chair across from the couch where Chloe was and re-filled Chloe's teacup.

"You haven't tried one of my scones," Sugar chastised, taking a second for herself.

Chloe had been hoping that her friend wouldn't notice. "I'm sorry, Sugar, they look delicious but I just don't think I can eat anything."

"Because of Reid," Sugar said knowingly. "So are you going to tell me what happened or leave me dying of curiosity?"

Chloe had to laugh at that. Clearly her friend had only been biding her time. "Did you just ask me out here today to get the inside story?" she joked.

"No, I asked you out here today because I thought you might need to talk. And because maybe I can help."

"Help?"

"Oh, Chloe, don't mess this up again," Sugar beseeched.

That surprised Chloe. "Don't mess this up again?" she repeated.

"Things with you and Reid. You two belong together."

"This isn't high school, Sugar," Chloe felt inclined to remind her friend.

"Well, you must think it is if you're so ready to throw this away again, as if you can both just cool off and then get back together after spring break."

"What am I throwing away again and how come you're so sure it's me who's doing it?" Chloe asked a bit defensively.

"You're throwing away Reid and I know it's you who's doing it because after all these years of Reid carrying a torch for you, if you aren't getting back together now, it's not because of him."

Chloe reminded herself that before this trip it had been a long time since she'd seen or spoken to Sugar, while Sugar had gone on living in the close community of Northbridge. So maybe now Sugar was more a friend to Reid than to her....

"It's complicated, Sugar," she said.

"How?"

"It just is."

"Tell me how," Sugar insisted. "It was complicated when you were kids. When you were still under the control of your parents. When you didn't want to go against them. But how is it complicated now?"

Chloe debated about whether or not to lay it all out for Sugar. On the one hand it wasn't any of Sugar's business and if she was on Reid's side, Chloe wasn't inclined to confide in her.

But on the other hand, Chloe had left Northbridge once before feeling like some kind of pariah. And while she now knew that that had been what her mother had made her believe because it had served her parents' purposes, she didn't particularly care to leave feeling that way a second time. She wanted at least Sugar to know that she had good reasons for turning down Reid's offer of a future together.

So she opted for telling Sugar the whole story.

And was surprised yet again when she'd finished and Sugar said, "You're right, Chloe. I don't think a person *can* talk themselves out of genuinely bad feelings toward someone else."

"Thank you. Now will you tell Reid that?"

"I don't think that's what Reid did."

"Oh, Sugar," Chloe said with a sigh, thinking that her moment of believing her old friend might have switched to her side had passed.

"I think," Sugar continued, "that what Reid did was talk himself *into* being mad and resentful fourteen years ago but that for the most part, that isn't how he's felt so he didn't need to talk himself out of it."

"How do you think he's felt for fourteen years? Because believe me, the person I met in the emergency room last Sunday night certainly *looked* like someone who was holding that grudge against me that you said yourself Reid was holding."

"He's a man, Chloe," Sugar said as if that explained it. "He was hurt. Really, really hurt. You know how men are—they can handle being really, really ticked off. But being hurt? They're a whole lot worse at dealing with that. They can't show it or they think they'll look weak. So they show something else—they get full of rage and indignation and all that other stuff. But underneath it? That man has loved you, plain and simple. Why else would it have been so easy for him to fall again just this past week? That's what he's held on to for fourteen years. The rest was just his cover and we've all known it all along."

Chloe didn't know what to say to that. She was too busy trying not to rush into believing it. So she only hedged. "I don't know about that, Sugar."

"I do," Sugar said confidently. "And I'll tell you something else, I know all about you, too."

Chloe laughed a little again. "What do you think you know about me?"

"I know your parents were difficult. I know they were very, very hard on you. And I know you were always so afraid of crossing them, of getting into trouble, that I couldn't even get you to push your curfew by five minutes or stop for a donut if you hadn't told your mother ahead of time that we might."

Chloe frowned. "What does that have to do with anything?"

"I know that Reid was the only one you ever stepped out of bounds with or for—I couldn't believe it when you told me you'd lost your virginity to him. *You!* I knew then that you had it bad for him. But when you got pregnant, that was the ultimate stepping out of bounds and you were scared to death of how your parents were going to react, and I understood that. I wouldn't have wanted to tell my parents I was pregnant at seventeen but I don't know what I would have done if I'd had to tell *your* parents."

Chloe had to laugh just a bit again at the look of horror on Sugar's face. "It was bad," she confirmed.

"And I know your life had to get a whole lot worse after that."

"The reins were definitely not loosened," Chloe understated.

"And here's what I think," Sugar continued. "I think that they had you so indoctrinated, so afraid of them, even before the pregnancy, that maybe afterward, once they had you away from Northbridge and Reid, you just got too afraid."

"Too afraid," Chloe repeated her old friend's words once more in order to have them clarified.

"Yes, too afraid. Too afraid of rocking the boat again. Probably too afraid that if you did, you'd lose your whole family—"

"They told me if I ever had another thing to do with Reid they'd never speak to me again, and they would have done it," Chloe repeated what she'd told Reid earlier in the week.

"And that's awful. I can't imagine what I would have felt or done if my folks had said that to me and I'd believed it was true. So it's understandable that you got too afraid. Too afraid of coming back here and having people say bad things about you. Too afraid of what they might have thought about you. But still, *too* afraid isn't a good thing, Chlo."

For some reason, what Sugar was saying and that last shortening of Chloe's name the way Sugar had when they were girls made Chloe's eyes fill again. And even though she blinked back the moisture, she stopped thinking that Sugar wasn't on her side because her old friend had teared up herself and was trying to regain her own control.

"Don't cry," Chloe cajoled with as much humor as she could muster. "I had enough trouble stopping to drive out here and if you get me started again I'll never get back."

"Good! Then I'll keep you here until I can make you see how things really are," Sugar said.

After another moment's struggle, they both managed to contain their emotions and then Sugar went on.

"And what I think," she said, "is that being too afraid left you too cautious. It left you playing it too safe. Too safe then to come back to Reid—although like I said, I can understand it when you were just a kid and faced losing your family—but too safe then and now."

"You think I'm playing it too safe now."

"I think if you're honestly turning Reid down now

because you're worried that he'll go on resenting what happened fourteen years ago, then yes, you're playing it too safe. Of course, if you're turning him down because he's right about you not having the same feelings for him…" Sugar smiled sadly. "Well, that's a whole other story."

Sugar stood suddenly. "And that's all I think," she concluded.

"That's enough," Chloe joked, not knowing what to say once more.

But apparently Sugar wasn't waiting for her to make any comment because she said, "Why don't I show you our new piglets? They're adorable."

For a moment Chloe sat there slightly dazed both by all her friend had said and by the abrupt change of subjects.

But then it sunk in that Sugar had given her a whole lot to think about and wasn't asking to know what her feelings for Reid were, that Sugar was leaving that for Chloe alone to sort out, to keep to herself.

So Chloe stood, too. "Okay, show me the piglets," she said.

But after what Sugar had just bombarded her with, Chloe doubted she was going to be able to concentrate on baby farm animals.

It was nearly 7:30 Sunday evening before Sugar would let Chloe leave. And that was only after Sugar had called her husband, Hank, to bring home pizza for dinner so Chloe could meet their three-year-old and five-year-old sons.

Chloe was glad she got to see the boys, but doubted she was very good company and so finally persuaded Sugar that she needed to go.

"Are you mad that I shot off my mouth?" Sugar asked as she walked Chloe to the rental car.

"No," Chloe answered without hesitation because of all the things churning inside her, anger at Sugar wasn't one of them.

"I'm keeping my fingers crossed," Sugar said then. "I'd like it if you were back in Northbridge to stay. You know we're having a girl this time," she added, placing a hand on her protruding stomach. "It'd be nice if you could be her godmother. And Reid could be her god-father…"

Chloe laughed at her friend's tenacity and got behind the steering wheel. "Good night, Sugar," was all she said in response.

"Remember—you've played it safe long enough," Sugar countered, closing the car door for her and stepping back to watch Chloe start the engine and pull away from the house.

As she did, Chloe thought about her old friend's theory that she'd played it too safe in the past. That she was playing it too safe with Reid now.

She knew she wasn't what anyone would consider a risk taker. The straight and narrow—that's what her father had hammered into her—*stick to the straight and narrow*….

And she had.

Well, with the exception of losing her virginity to Reid and getting pregnant.

But Sugar was right, before the pregnancy Chloe had never bent the rules, let alone broken them.

Her parents just hadn't been like Sugar's parents or like Reid's widowed mom. Chloe had had much more to contend with even before the pregnancy had happened.

Then the pregnancy *had* happened.

And everything about her parents' reaction had been out of proportion—accusations that she'd ruined her father's political career and her parents' lives, that none of them would ever be able to hold their heads up in Northbridge again, that she'd turned herself into damaged goods that no man would ever want.

No question, out of proportion.

So, had she played it safe after that?

Absolutely.

Had she been even more afraid of rocking the boat after that?

Actually, she'd been terrified.

Only now she had to wonder *why* she should have been terrified.

Had her own fears grown out of proportion as some kind of response to her parents' out-of-proportion expectations of her and reactions to nearly everything, but certainly to the pregnancy? Because of that, after the pregnancy, had she played it all the more safe than she had even as a kid who went home early rather than risk missing a single curfew?

Was she so accustomed to playing it too safe that she was refusing herself a future with Reid now?

It actually seemed possible to her.

She knew she'd always played it safer than anyone else. That she'd had few friends in school because only Sugar had had the patience for her fretting over every rule and her determination never to do anything she wasn't supposed to. She knew that after the pregnancy, even in college, she'd lived at home because her parents had still wanted to keep tabs on her and she'd let them rather than moving out. She knew she hadn't dated a single person after Reid that she'd thought they wouldn't approve of and, in fact, hadn't been really willing to let any relationship go beyond a date or two until Thad— the man her mother and father had *wanted* her to be with, the man she'd stayed with even though her own feelings for him had been wishy-washy. She knew she'd played it safe in her job, that she'd turned down a better offer from another company to stay where she was because she'd been too worried about making a change.

That all seemed like playing it awfully safe. Too safe.

Or was *she* just talking herself out of and into something?

She gave that serious consideration.

But even looking at it from every angle, she couldn't convince herself that she was merely talking herself into or out of anything. It seemed more that, with Sugar's help, she was finally seeing the whole picture. Seeing her own actions more clearly. She thought she was finally opening her eyes to things like why she had stayed with Thad for eight years when, deep down, it had been Reid she'd dreamed of and fantasized about. Reid who had continued all this time to slip into her thoughts. Reid who she'd wanted.

And maybe if Reid was who she'd wanted all along, she could believe that she was who he'd wanted all along, too...

Except that there was still the issue of his hard feelings towards her. Hard feelings she hadn't had toward him.

Had Sugar been right about that, too? she asked herself. Were Reid's hard feelings more a camouflage for his softer feelings for her?

It would have been nice to buy into that. But Chloe couldn't. Even if she could write off the resentment and anger she'd seen in him as a cover, she'd still hurt him—Sugar had said it herself. Chloe had really, really hurt him. And hurt was a very hard feeling.

Which left her, she decided, needing to gauge which of Reid's feelings for her might be stronger—the good ones or the bad ones. And which had the most potential for winning out in the long run.

Her thoughts went to Thad again because when it had come to Thad, the bad feelings she'd had for him had won out.

But now that she was seeing that relationship more clearly, she knew that that was because the bad feelings were stronger. That the love she'd felt for Thad had never been near to what she'd felt for Reid. So of course the bad had won out.

But with Reid? Could she hope that if he'd gone on carrying a torch for her all this time—as Sugar had claimed—that the good feelings were stronger? That if she just gave their relationship the opportunity, the good feelings would prevail from here on?

It was risky. And no matter how much her eyes had been opened to why and how much she'd played it safe until now, it was difficult for her to accept any kind of risk.

Chloe drove by the turnoff to the old bridge just then and out of the blue she thought about the reverend's wife and all the talk that was going on about Celeste and the bank robbers.

Chloe was struck again with sympathy for the woman who had made a mistake and paid for it in horrible regret.

But something else hit her, too.

She couldn't say that she regretted not coming back to Reid fourteen years ago because she couldn't regret not doing something she hadn't felt free to do in the first place.

Only now she *was* free. Free not to play it *too* safe. Free not to let her fears and worries be out of proportion. And if she left Reid this time? If she didn't gamble on the good feelings and the chance that those good feelings might be what they got to share for the rest of their lives?

That she knew she would regret.

That she knew she would never stop regretting.

Because while Reid had worried that her feelings for him hadn't been equal to his for her, while Sugar had questioned it, too, neither of them could be more wrong.

There had never been anyone else for Chloe. There never would be anyone else for her. Because there just wasn't any room left in her heart for anyone but him.

And since that was the case…

She realized there was only one way for her to go.

No matter how much it scared her, no matter how unfamiliar and rattling it was to her, this time she couldn't play it too safe.

This time she couldn't play it safe at all.

But as unnerving as that was to her, what occurred to her then was even worse.

What if this time had been one time too many for her to have hurt Reid?

Chapter Fourteen

Having made up her mind about Reid, Chloe, was torn as she pulled the rental car into her driveway at home. A part of her wanted to rush across the street to talk to him. But another part of her knew she'd likely be encountering the hostility she'd met a week ago at this time and she wasn't eager for that.

So, procrastinating, she went into her own house first, only casting a glance across the street and noting that there were lights on behind the closed drapes of the living room and that Reid's car was parked at the curb.

At least he was home, she thought, going upstairs to her bedroom once she was inside.

It wouldn't do any harm to look good, she told herself. And with that in mind she surveyed the clothes she'd brought with her.

If she were at her apartment in Tucson, with her entire wardrobe to pick from, she knew exactly what she would have worn. But as it was, her choices were limited.

She opted for a white cardigan sweater because she could leave enough buttons open from the neckline down to add the allure she was after. A little cleavage—distraction from Reid's most recent round of anger and disappointment was in order, she thought.

Then she changed out of the baggy, weekend jeans she'd worn for her visit with Sugar and into the pair she'd brought with Reid in mind in the first place. The jeans that did wonders for her rear end.

With her clothes taken care of, she went into the bathroom. She hadn't felt up to putting on makeup earlier in the day and without any to wash off she merely held a cold washcloth to her face and eyes in an attempt to bring down some of the redness and swelling left by crying so much in the last day and a half. It helped some and when it had she dried her face and applied blush and several layers of mascara.

Lip gloss finished that portion of Reid-readiness, leaving only her hair to be revamped.

She removed the clip that had held it in a ponytail, bent over at the waist, and brushed from her scalp outward until her wavy locks were refluffed. Upright again, she tossed her head and made some adjustments to a curl here and there with her fingers until she had the coal-black strands exactly where she wanted them.

After one final assessment of the whole picture in the bathroom mirror she judged herself presentable.

Which meant that the moment had arrived.

"If you want him, you're gonna have to go get him," she told her reflection.

And since there was no doubt that she wanted Reid, she took several deep breaths to try to gain some calm, and retraced her steps out of the house to go across the street.

Her hand was shaking as she rang the doorbell and only when she had did she realize that she didn't have any idea what she was going to say to Reid.

A wave of panic surged through her at that thought and for a moment she considered diving into the bushes rather than going through with this unprepared.

But just then the door opened and it was too late.

It also wasn't Reid who opened the door.

It was Luke.

It didn't help her stress level any to have to face Reid's brother. In fact, it was even more embarrassing. And Luke didn't seem all that welcoming since he frowned and said a surprised and ominous-sounding, "Chloe."

"Is Reid here?" she blurted out, feeling like a backward teenager.

Luke shook his head, making things worse because Chloe didn't know if he was leading up to telling her Reid wasn't there or that Reid wouldn't see her even if he was.

Then he said, "He's up the street. Mom has a plugged drain."

So Reid wasn't home. That was better than a refusal to see her. But not a lot better when her courage was waning by the minute.

"If something is wrong at your place—a clogged drain or something—I can take care of it," Luke added.

But why? Chloe wondered. Was Luke only being helpful? Or was he running interference to keep her away from Reid? There was no way of knowing so Chloe continued despite her own growing insecurities.

"No, nothing's wrong with the house. I just wanted…needed…to talk to him."

Luke nodded somberly. "He's not in a good mood."

"I'm sure. But would you have him come over as soon as he gets done at your mom's anyway?"

Luke scratched the corner of his eye. "I can relay the message. I can't promise he'll come."

So it was the worst of what she'd feared—Reid didn't want anything to do with her.

Crestfallen, Chloe reminded herself that he had good cause and said, "If you'd just tell him."

"I will."

"Thanks."

There was no more to say, so Chloe turned on her heels and went back across the street.

She told herself as she did that at least maybe now she could think about what to say to Reid.

But once she got inside again, that wasn't what she did. She couldn't.

All she could do was stand in the shadows of the living room where no one could see her from outside, watch Reid and Luke's house, and worry that she really had ruined her life this time. That she was going to have to go through with the closing tomorrow and return to Arizona knowing that—once too often—she'd pushed away the man she wanted and lost him for good. That no man would ever compare to him. That she would live the rest of her years alone and lonely and regretting that she'd been so stupid and afraid and—

And then there he was!

Walking from his mother's house to his own.

Tall, lean, powerfully handsome, and definitely without any sign that he felt as bad as she did, or that he was the basket case she was.

Maybe because he'd finally, once and for all, put her behind him....

Chloe watched him as he went up to his house, feasting on the sight of him from the rear, on the way his jeans rode his terrific derriere, on the way his back formed a vee from narrow waist to expansive shoulders encased in a white Henley T-shirt, and she wondered how she would ever be able to stand it if she couldn't convince him she'd changed her mind.

He went into his house and closed the door.

And Chloe waited.

And waited and waited.

A full half hour went by and put her in even more of a panic.

What if Luke hadn't told Reid that she wanted to talk to him? Maybe Luke didn't approve. He certainly hadn't seemed any too thrilled to see her.

Or maybe Luke had told Reid and Reid had just blown it off. Maybe Reid had said he didn't care what she had to say or why she wanted to see him, that he was finished with her....

She didn't know what to do.

She didn't know if she should go across the street again. If she should call. If she should merely wait and hope.

But what if she waited the whole night and Reid never showed up and then she had to see him at the closing tomorrow morning?

There were just no good possibilities. And the longer she went without a single hint of anything happening across the street, the more distraught she felt.

Maybe I should call Sugar. Maybe she has an idea...

Just as desperation set in, the front door opened on Reid's house and out he came.

He hadn't used the time to change clothes the way she had, so she knew he hadn't merely been sprucing up. And his expression was dark. Dark and forbidding—like he was doing something he was loath to do.

This can't go well...

When he reached her front door he didn't use his key and come in. He rang the bell.

Chloe swallowed her own fear of rejection, took yet another deep breath, and went to open the door.

"Hi," she said, sounding as winded as if she'd just run a marathon, her voice small and uncertain.

"Luke said you wanted something."

No doubt about it, this was the Reid she'd met at the emergency room a week ago. Curt, cold, giving no quarter.

But Chloe reminded herself that it was no more than she'd expected. No more than she deserved.

She stepped out of the doorway, and said, "Come in. Please."

He didn't accept the invitation immediately. In fact he stood where he was on the front stoop for so long she began to wonder if he was that reluctant or if his actions were a refusal all on their own.

But then he finally drew in a breath that seemed disgusted, and came inside.

Chloe closed the door and turned to find him going far enough to peer into the kitchen.

Probably because he preferred looking there than at her.

Then he said, "I don't know why you want me over here except maybe to say you hope we can be friends or to find out if I'm all right or some touchy-feely garbage like that to make yourself feel better. But if that's the case, let's save it."

"That's not the case," Chloe said, staring at the back he was still presenting to her. Then, with the last ounce of courage she could muster, she added, "Well, the part about my wanting you is the case, but the rest isn't."

Reid glanced over his shoulder at her, seemed to digest her words, and only after he had did he pivot enough to face her.

"Wanting me for what?" he demanded with one arched eyebrow and a tough-enough tone not to leave her with any illusions that that was all she had to say.

Chloe shrugged. "For everything. Forever."

Her heart was beating so hard and fast when she said that that she thought he could probably hear it despite the fact that several feet separated them.

"That's a switch," he commented, only a shade less harshly. "How did that happen?"

"With Sugar's help. She gave me a good talking-to this afternoon."

Chloe went on to tell him all that their mutual friend had said and the conclusions she'd come to after considering Sugar's points of view.

"I don't think she's right about everything," Chloe said at the end. "I don't think that the rotten things you've felt—and are probably feeling now—are just what you're using to cover your other feelings because you're a man. But what I'm hoping is that maybe the other feelings are strong enough and real enough to overrule the rotten ones."

"Unlike your *other* feelings for Thad?"

"Yes," she said without reservation. "That was part of what I realized on my way home from Sugar's—that the *stronger* feelings and not necessarily just the bad ones are what end up ruling. My resentment was stronger than anything else I felt for Thad. I'm hoping that might not be true for you."

"Why are you hoping that? So we can be *friends?*" he asked as if he were challenging her.

"I think you know why," she said, not wanting to go too far out on a limb when she wasn't yet sure if things between them were redeemable.

But then it occurred to her that her feelings for him were *his* issue—that he didn't think she cared about him as much as he cared about her. So she shouldn't expect—or even hope—that he might let this go in the direction she was aiming for without hearing exactly how she felt about him.

So she resigned herself to going out on that limb

after all, and said, "I decided Sugar was wrong about your feelings and you're wrong about mine. I love you, Reid. I loved you when we were kids. I've loved you ever since—which was why I had so much trouble committing to Thad and why the bad things he'd made me feel were stronger than the good."

She wasn't actually looking at Reid as she said that because she was taking a risk, and watching his reaction—which might be negative—was more than she could make herself do.

But now she forced her eyes to meet his, risking everything when she said, "And all it took was seeing you again now, being with you, to let me know that I'm still in love with you. Head-over-heels, crazy, wild in love with you. Enough in love with you that I'm willing to take the chance that you love me more than you hate me."

"Hate you," he repeated. "I don't think I've ever—*ever*—said I hate you. Or even thought it. I hated that you left Northbridge. I hated that you didn't come back with me from Tucson. I hated that you *weren't* willing to take the chance on me yesterday. But I have never hated you."

She hoped that was true. And that hating things she had and hadn't done wasn't the same thing as hating her. But she was also very aware of the fact that he hadn't said he loved her, either....

And she didn't know what more to say herself, so she just stood there, watching him and waiting again.

His green eyes didn't waver from hers as he seemed to be searching for reassurance that she meant what she said.

She couldn't blame him for not being sure of her.

Every time he had been in the past she'd pulled the rug out from under him.

But then she saw the expression on that face she adored ease up and a small smile took the corners of his mouth.

"It's about time," he said with a sigh that sounded relieved.

"I know."

"Now tell me where we're going with this."

He really was wary of her. But she wasn't willing to take *all* the risks. At least not alone.

"Where do you want it to go?" she countered.

His eyebrows arched. "I want you to marry me," he said as if that were obvious. "The sooner the better. I want you to live with me in Northbridge and be a part of everything here and have kids and never leave me again. I want us to die when we're a hundred and ten holding hands."

"Okay."

"Okay?" he repeated. "That's it? Just *okay?*"

"I'd like it if you told me you honestly do think you can shake off the hard feelings because you love me, too. Because in everything you've said to me, you've measured feelings and had mine coming up short of yours, but I've yet to hear you say—"

"I love you, Chloe," he cut her off, moving from where he stood in the center of the room to stand directly in front of her, to pull her to him with his hands at the sides of her waist. "I have always loved you and I always will love you. I just didn't know what it was going to take to make you admit that you loved me, too. Apparently I should have enlisted Sugar's voice of reason a long time ago."

"It might have saved us a lot of grief," Chloe agreed, raising her palms to his pectorals and allowing herself to begin to absorb the fact that this just might work out after all.

"I do love you, Reid," she said, her voice cracking for no reason she understood.

"I might need you to say that ten or twelve times a day."

"To chase away the bad feelings?"

He grinned down at her. "No, just because I like hearing it. Sugar wasn't completely wrong about the bad feelings—they were kind of a way to cope with loving you and not having you. A way to tough it out. So shaking them isn't too complicated now that I do have you."

He kissed her then—a full, deep kiss that helped to convince her that he genuinely wasn't harboring any hard feelings.

Well, except maybe the one that was beginning to nudge her below the waist....

But Reid wasn't the only one of them that that kiss was inspiring. It was igniting in Chloe, too, everything that had been alive in her on Friday night.

She tried not to show it, though, when the kiss ended. Instead she looked into the face she was only too happy to look at for eternity and said, "So we're engaged?"

"Oh, yeah," he answered, kissing her again.

"And I'm moving back to Northbridge?"

"Will you?"

"Yes," she said without having to consider it because she realized suddenly that coming back to the small town had not only not been as difficult as she'd feared, its charm and warmth made it exactly where she wanted to be. As long as she was with Reid. "I'm not sure what will happen with work—if I can freelance or—"

"Details—we'll sort through them later," he said, kissing her yet again as if that was all that was really important.

And certainly, to Chloe, too, that was all that *was* really important at that moment.

So that was what she gave her thoughts and herself over to—kissing him in return, parting her lips in answer to his, meeting his tongue when it came to toy with hers, and raising her hands to the solid column of his neck and into his hair.

And just as it had after the wedding, passion began there near the doorway, sparking immediately hot and moving them again to Chloe's bedroom.

Clothes were thrown off as fast as they could be and without any awareness of how they got there because her attention was consumed by Reid, Chloe found herself on the bed with him.

As hungry for each other as if they hadn't been apart only since the morning before, hands and mouths explored and aroused and pleased with abandon. Nothing was held back, no inhibitions showed themselves and together they made turbulent love in a haze of desire that couldn't be tamed.

Together they reached peaks that, for Chloe, was a culmination so acute she couldn't imagine ever again being without the man who had brought it to life within her.

Afterwards they collapsed into a heap of entwined limbs and satiated, still-joined bodies, with Reid on his back and Chloe atop him, using his shoulder as a pillow.

"And you were even *thinking* about walking away from this?" Reid joked in a gravely voice.

Chloe laughed a little. "I must have been out of my mind," she agreed.

"You weren't just leading me on with that other stuff to get me into bed before you disappear into the wilds of Arizona again, were you?"

"You've discovered my secret!"

He pulsed inside her. "Not to mention a few other things."

Chloe grinned up at him and did all she had the energy for—she kissed the underside of his chin. "Actually, the fourteen-year hiatus might have been worth it just for what you've learned about this since our first time," she said, pushing her hips into him.

"Nah, nothing was worth that. Look at all of this that we've missed." Another pulse.

"We'll just have to do everything we can to make up for lost time."

"Great idea!" he decreed.

But none of the making-up-for-lost-time was going to happen at that moment because his eyes drifted heavily down and Chloe felt him relaxing.

"Are you falling asleep on me?" she asked, pretending to be put out.

"I believe *you're* on *me*," he said, tightening his arms around her so she couldn't move. "And I promise I'll only sleep for a little while. I didn't get any last night."

"Here I thought I was marrying a tireless superstud."

"Give me half an hour," he said thickly, one hand

coming up to cup her head, to weave his fingers into her hair in a lulling kind of massage that was making sleep irresistible to Chloe, too.

So she fitted her cheek into the hollow of his shoulder again and closed her eyes, feeling incredibly weary, incredibly content, incredibly happy.

And in that moment she indulged in something she'd never been able to do before.

She indulged herself in the sure and certain knowledge that when she woke up again, Reid Walker would still be there. That he would always be there for her, just as she would always be there for him.

And nothing else—not anything that had happened in the past, not anything that either of them had ever felt—mattered.

"I love you, Reid," she whispered, even though she knew he was asleep.

And she planned to prove just how much she loved him every day for the rest of her life.

* * * * *

Coming in October 2006,
Victoria Pade presents IT TAKES A FAMILY,
the next installment in her
NORTHBRIDGE NUPTIALS *miniseries.*
You won't want to miss learning more about
Reverend Perry's wife and
the decades-old robbery that
still remains unsolved!

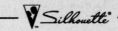

SPECIAL EDITION™

COMING IN SEPTEMBER FROM
USA TODAY **BESTSELLING AUTHOR**

SUSAN MALLERY

THE LADIES' MAN

Rachel Harper wondered how she'd tell
Carter Brockett the news—their spontaneous
night of passion had left her pregnant!
What would he think of the naive
schoolteacher who'd lost control? After
all, the man had a legion of exes who'd
been unable to snare a commitment, and
here she had a forever-binding one!

Then she remembered.
He'd lost control, too....

positively
+pregnant

***Sometimes the unexpected
is the best news of all...***

**Introducing an exciting appearance
by legendary
New York Times bestselling author**

DIANA PALMER

HEARTBREAKER

He's the ultimate bachelor…
but he may have just met
the one woman to change his ways!

Join the drama in the story of a confirmed
bachelor, an amnesiac beauty and their
unexpected passionate romance.

**"Diana Palmer is a mesmerizing storyteller
who captures the essence of what
a romance should be."—*Affaire de Coeur***

**Heartbreaker *is available from Silhouette Desire
in September 2006.***

If you enjoyed what you just read,
then we've got an offer you can't resist!

Take 2 bestselling
love stories FREE!
Plus get a FREE surprise gift!

Clip this page and mail it to Silhouette Reader Service™

IN U.S.A.	IN CANADA
3010 Walden Ave.	P.O. Box 609
P.O. Box 1867	Fort Erie, Ontario
Buffalo, N.Y. 14240-1867	L2A 5X3

YES! Please send me 2 free Silhouette Special Edition® novels and my free surprise gift. After receiving them, if I don't wish to receive anymore, I can return the shipping statement marked cancel. If I don't cancel, I will receive 6 brand-new novels every month, before they're available in stores! In the U.S.A., bill me at the bargain price of $4.24 plus 25¢ shipping and handling per book and applicable sales tax, if any*. In Canada, bill me at the bargain price of $4.99 plus 25¢ shipping and handling per book and applicable taxes**. That's the complete price and a savings of at least 10% off the cover prices—what a great deal! I understand that accepting the 2 free books and gift places me under no obligation ever to buy any books. I can always return a shipment and cancel at any time. Even if I never buy another book from Silhouette, the 2 free books and gift are mine to keep forever.

235 SDN DZ9D
335 SDN DZ9E

Name	(PLEASE PRINT)	
Address	Apt.#	
City	State/Prov.	Zip/Postal Code

Not valid to current Silhouette Special Edition® subscribers.

Want to try two free books from another series?
Call 1-800-873-8635 or visit www.morefreebooks.com.

* Terms and prices subject to change without notice. Sales tax applicable in N.Y.
** Canadian residents will be charged applicable provincial taxes and GST.
   All orders subject to approval. Offer limited to one per household.
   ® are registered trademarks owned and used by the trademark owner and or its licensee.

SPED04R   ©2004 Harlequin Enterprises Limited

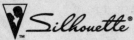
SPECIAL EDITION

#1777 MARRIED IN HASTE—Christine Rimmer
Bravo Family Ties
When it came to grand fiery passions, Angie Dellazola had been there, done that—and been burned. Marrying steady-minded hometown boy Brett Bravo seemed like the ticket to the quiet life…until pent-up passions exploded between the unsuspecting newlyweds!

#1778 THE LADIES' MAN—Susan Mallery
Positively Pregnant
Rachel Harper wasn't the one-night-stand type, but when sexy Carter Brockett offered the stranded kindergarten teacher a ride, one thing led to another.… And now Rachel had news for the ladies' man—she was pregnant….

#1779 EXPECTING HIS BROTHER'S BABY—
Karen Rose Smith
Baby Bonds
When Brock Warner returned to Saddle Ridge, he found the family ranch falling to pieces, its custodian—his pregnant, recently widowed sister-in-law, Kylie Armstrong Warner—in the hospital, and his own long-buried feelings for her resurfacing in a big way….

#1780 A LITTLE CHANGE OF PLANS—Jen Safrey
Talk of the Neighborhood
Pregnant after a college reunion fling, consultant Molly Jackson's business and reputation were on the line. So she turned to her laid-back best friend Adam Shibbs for a cover-up marriage of convenience—but would real love spring from their short-term charade?

#1781 UNDER THE WESTERN SKY—Laurie Paige
Canyon Country
When mild-mannered midwife Julianne Martin was accused of trafficking stolen Native American artifacts, Park Service investigator Tony Aquilon realized he had the wrong woman…or *did* he?

#1782 THE RIGHT BROTHER—Patricia McLinn
Seasons in a Small Town
A deadbeat ex had left Jennifer Truesdale and her daughter high and dry—until her ex's brother, Trent Stenner, saved the day, buying out the family car dealership and giving Jennifer a job. But was the former football pro just making a pass at this lady in distress?